CASTAWAYS

CASTAWAYS

DAVID MCDONALD

JOE BOOKS LTD

Published simultaneously in the United States and Canada
by Joe Books Ltd, 567 Queen St. West, Toronto, ON M5V 2B6

www.joebooks.com

Library and Archives Canada Cataloguing in Publication
information is available upon request.

ISBN 978-1-772752-04-5 (print)
ISBN 978-1-988032-31-3 (ebook)

First Joe Books Edition: April 2016
3 5 7 9 10 8 6 4 2 1

Printed and bound in Canada

To my Muse. You know who you are.

He stands in the middle of the cleared space that acts as their arena, the avid faces of the crowd staring down at him. He is their champion, and he can feel them willing him on. They have never seen him beaten, and they cannot believe that tonight could be the night that he meets his match.

But he is not alone in the ring. Towering over him is the huge figure he must overcome. He has faced bigger men, and he has faced faster men, but he doesn't think that he has ever faced a man as big and as fast as this one, and the unshakable aura of self-belief he carries around with him wherever he goes is starting to fade.

He is covered in bruises, and the way that pain stabs through his side whenever he moves is worrying him—it feels like at least one rib is broken. Blood drips from a cut on his brow, and he blinks it away from his eyes, cursing at the sting. His vision is starting to blur, but still he looks around the crowd, searching for a friendly face.

There are many that are familiar—some with whom he has become very familiar indeed—but none of the faces he needs to see are there. There is the Duke who has become his patron, the Duke's councillors, the Duke's beautiful daughter. But the friends with whom he has faced a hundred life-or-death situations are absent, and they are the ones he needs now.

As his gigantic opponent closes in, Peter Quill wonders how it has come to this; how he has found himself in a strange land, surrounded by strangers, all alone, and without those who mean the most to him.

CHAPTER 1

One moment they were arguing, the next they were being flung from side to side in the spaceship, caroming off the walls in a mad version of table tennis, a game from Earth that Peter Quill remembered only vaguely from his childhood.

"It wasn't my fault," Quill had protested, sparking the argument.

The rest of his companions glared at him—other than Groot who was looking out the spaceship window, a happy smile on his face.

"Not your fault?" Rocket Raccoon asked incredulously. "How do you figure that?"

"How could I have known that our client would prove to be such an ingrate? We rescued his only daughter and heir from space pirates, and did so before they could harm a hair on her head or threaten her virtue."

"That might have carried more weight with him if the pirates were the *real* threat to her virtue," Gamora said drily. She was a beautiful young woman with green skin, but the knives at her sides showed signs of hard use, and belied her youthful appearence. "Not quite what they mean by setting a thief to catch a robber."

"Our client's daughter was a robber?" Drax asked. "I did not know this."

"No, you idiot," Rocket snapped. "It's a proverb."

"I don't understand," Drax rumbled, a hint of anger in his voice. He was intimidating at the best of times, his green skin marked with the scars of countless battles, and his massive body bulging with muscles. Even when he sounded happy, he made you nervous, and right now he was downright scary. "Call me an idiot again and I'll squash you, rodent."

Rocket snarled at him, but Gamora broke in before Rocket could say anything to further inflame the situation.

"It's an old saying, Drax. It means that the best person to catch a robber is another thief, because they know what to look for," she explained gently. "I was trying to make a play on words that insinuated sending Quill to save our client's daughter was like sending a thief to catch another thief because . . ." She sighed. "These things are never funny when you have to explain them."

"I still don't understand," Drax complained.

"You wouldn't," Rocket muttered, and then more loudly, "But that's not the point. The point is Quill's inability to resist a pretty face nearly got us arrested—again—and also cost us a small fortune in credits."

"Hey, wait a minute!" Quill protested. "*I* wasn't the one who blew a hole in the side of our client's mansion. I'm sure we could have talked it through if you'd just given me a chance!"

"I think the time for talking had well and truly passed by then," Rocket said. "Or maybe I was reading too much into the fact that he had set his own private army on us, and that they were shooting in our direction?"

"We'll have to agree to disagree," Quill said.

"This is not humorous," Drax said. "This is yet another example of your lack of self-discipline causing trouble for us. A warrior must learn to master himself before he can master others."

Quill opened his mouth, but his reply died unsaid when he saw the others nodding their heads.

"You all feel this way?" Quill asked, looking at each of them. "Rocket?"

"Sorry, Quill, but you're not always thinking with your brain, if you know what I mean."

Quill flushed. "Gamora?"

"Quill, I've come to accept that you can't help yourself when it comes to women," she said gently. "I'm sure you mean the wonderful words you use, and that when you call them special and tell them that they are the only one, you really do mean it at the time—but you seem to have met a lot of special women."

"Groot?" There was a faintly imploring note in Quill's voice as he addressed the seven-foot-tall ambulatory tree. As usual, Groot had a slight smile on his face, and it was hard to know what he was thinking.

"I am Groot."

Quill didn't need Rocket to translate that—the expression of vindication on the raccoonoid's face told him that Groot wasn't on Quill's side.

"Well, I'm sorry you all feel that way," Quill said, starting to get angry. Their comments had cut uncomfortably close to the bone. "It's not like you all don't have your own flaws."

He pointed at Rocket. "You've got the worst case of little-man syndrome I have ever seen, and your answer to every problem seems to be to blow it up." He moved his finger to Gamora. "The only way *you* can interact with a guy is by trying to stab him." He moved along. "And you, Drax—telling the absolute truth is not always a virtue. Ever heard of little white lies? You can be pretty hurtful."

"I am Groot."

Quill's finger stabbed out. "And, you . . . you . . . you get leaves absolutely everywhere in my ship!"

Quill's anger suddenly deflated as he realized how ridiculous he sounded. His shoulders slumped and he stared at the floor, not wanting to meet anyone's eyes. They were right, of course. He had been selfish and had put himself before the team. He would love to tell them it would never happen again, but that would be more than a little white lie.

"Well, I think Quill makes some good points," Gamora said, surprising him. "I am sick of all this arguing, and people doing whatever they want to or whatever they think is a good idea at the time. Maybe it's time for a break."

"A break?" Quill and Rocket said at the same time, then glared at each other.

"What do you mean, a break?" the raccoon-like creature asked.

"Exactly that," Gamora said. "We've been cooped up together for much too long, and I think we're starting to get on each other's nerves. Perhaps it's time to go our separate ways."

She held up a hand to forestall their protests, all of them trying to talk at once.

"I don't mean for good, but some time away from each other could be beneficial. A holiday, nothing permanent," Gamora said. "We're not going to make back all the money we've lost on our own, right? I think Quill owes us a more . . . successful mission."

"Maybe that's not such a bad idea," Quill said thoughtfully, ignoring the dig. "We *have* been living in each other's pockets, haven't we? Not literally, Drax—I mean we haven't had much time to ourselves. A few months doing our own thing might help us appreciate each other a bit more. And when we're ready, we might find working together fun again."

"Yeah, I agree," Rocket said. "So, where would you go, Gamora?"

"Somewhere I could meditate in peace and quiet. Maybe

an uninhabited planet so I could have all the time alone I wanted," she said, sounding wistful. "I need to process some of the things I've seen and done lately, and I just want to clear my mind and find my center again."

"Borrrrring," Rocket said.

"Well, where would you go?" she asked. "Something tells me you won't be looking for a path to self-improvement."

"The only thing I'm looking to improve is my bank balance." He glared at Quill. "Due to the choices of certain people who will go nameless, it's looking pretty bleak right now. That's why I want to go to the casino planet, Sin. Every game of chance you can imagine, and some you can't. And the amount of money that flows through there . . ." he trailed off, a dreamy note in his voice.

"Yes, *your* money flowing to *them*," Gamora said.

"Not in this case!" Rocket said. "Groot and I have a system. Don't we, buddy?"

"I am Groot."

"See? We're going to win big, I guarantee it. And while we're there, I'm going to eat until I cannot move," Rocket said. "How about you, Drax? What do you do when you aren't busting heads?"

"I only have one interest, and that is pursuing vengeance for my family," Drax said, unsmiling. "If we take a break I will leave you to your childish entertainments and do what I have always done—search for justice."

"Drax, you are such a downer," Quill snapped. "Can't you let us just enjoy the moment or something?"

"Maybe if you worried less about your enjoyment and more about serious matters, we wouldn't find ourselves with no money and no prospects," Drax said.

"I'm not taking life advice from a guy who doesn't know what a proverb is."

"I don't need to know what a proverb is to snap you in half, Quill."

Gamora stepped between them. "That's enough—from both of you. I'm sick of having to be a mother to boys; it's not what I signed up for."

It was then that the ship began to shake and shudder. It was tossed around like a twig in a stream, spinning along every axis. There was no way to judge direction; one moment their feet were on the floor, the next their feet were on the ceiling—or on a wall. Every so often the ship would hit a pocket of turbulence and simply drop, the floor falling out from under them, leaving them feeling like their stomachs had been left behind. There was nothing Quill could do. He'd been thrown from his chair in the first few seconds, and even if he'd been able to reach the controls, the ship was in the grip of forces far more powerful than it could possibly compensate for—no matter how skillful the pilot.

Rocket handled the disruption most easily, leaping from body to body as they tumbled though the spacecraft. The genetically augmented creature may as well have been built for this, his animal reflexes allowing him to react to the pitching and yawing of the ship, his sharp claws digging into the walls—not to mention the clothing and skin of anyone unlucky to have him land on them. Quill could hear his shipmates cursing Rocket until finally he clung to Groot, who had braced himself in a corner, growing additional tendrils to anchor himself.

"What's going on?" yelled Gamora, trying to be heard above the wailing klaxon of the ship's alarm. The green-skinned warrior had managed to strap herself into the copilot's chair and was scanning the readouts displayed on the few screens that were still functioning.

Quill groped his way over to the console and pulled himself into the pilot's chair, quickly attaching the harness that he normally refused to wear. His fingers danced over the keypad as he grabbed the controls and, straining against the bucking ship, finally managed to bring it under control. The craft leveled out, but as it resumed its normal orientation there was a loud crash. Quill could hear Drax cursing—he must have been caught unawares when up became up once more—and down became down. Quill set the syscomp to run a diagnostic to check for any major damage, and then began to analyze the data coming from the external sensors that had survived whatever had hit them.

"There!" Quill pointed to one of the forward sensor displays. "See that?"

Gamora and Rocket crowded in behind him.

"I don't see anything," Rocket said at first. ". . . Ah, there it is. What the hell is it?"

The monitor showed a grandstand view of a vast nebula that coruscated with all the colors of the visible spectrum, and probably a whole lot more. But as glorious it was, the nebula was not what they were paying attention to. As they watched, a section of the view rippled, as if some transparent sheet of material had caught in the solar breeze. Adjusting for scale, they were focusing on an area of space the size of a small moon. Quill punched a button and the visual was overlaid with lines representing the local gravitational fields. When the lines passed through that section of space, they bent—significantly.

"Whatever that thing is, we must have gotten caught in its gravity well," Quill said. "That's what triggered the alarm and emergency evasion procedures. We should count ourselves lucky that we got off so easy."

"I think you may be overlooking something," Gamora said.

"What's that?" Quill asked.

"Have you ever seen that nebula before?" she asked. "It isn't on any of the charts we have."

Quill swore and looked at the ship's present coordinates. He had been so caught up in checking for damage that he hadn't even thought to check their location.

"According to these readings, we're . . . a little off course."

"How much is a little?" Gamora asked.

"Only about 350 light years," Quill said grimly.

"So where *are* we then?" Rocket was flipping through the battered ship's atlas. "I can't see that nebula anywhere."

Gamora was far better at astronavigation than Quill was, so he let her run the numbers.

"Bad news," she reported. "We are in uncharted space. Whatever that thing is, it must have thrown us out of hyperspace. We're lucky we came out intact, rather than as a spray of superheated plasma."

"That sounds like good news to me!" Quill said. "We're alive, and what's a few hundred light years? We'll be back on track before you know it."

Gamora was shaking her head before he had even finished.

"You need to read this damage report. Looks like one of the crystal arrays on the hyperdrive shattered. We aren't going anywhere soon."

Everyone started talking at once, drowning each other out in a cacophony of accusations and complaints. Finally, Quill raised his fingers to his lips and gave a short, sharp, and very piercing whistle.

"Calm down everyone. Let's not get carried away. The safety overrides are designed to kick in if the ship is about to drop out of hyperspace due to unforeseen factors—and to bring us out near the closest habitable planet. All we need to do is land there and find the materials we need, and then the ship will repair itself."

He looked around at them. "Okay?"

They all nodded, albeit a little sullenly.

"Gamora, is there anything on the sensors?"

She scanned them for a few moments before nodding.

"There we go," she said. "A 'G' class planet, gravity .8 Standard. Plenty of oxygen and incredibly clean air—I'm talking no traces of hydrocarbons at all. Decent climate, not holiday material but better than a lot I have seen." Her voice took on a note of excitement. "Preliminary scans of the crust show plenty of heavy metals. We'll have no trouble finding raw materials. There's only one real downside to the place."

"What's that?" Quill asked her.

"I'm not picking up any signs of even moderately advanced technology. No radio waves, and as I said, no hydrocarbons. No satellite network—in fact, not a single artificial structure in orbit." She ran her finger down the screen. "There is one area the scans can't penetrate—look, right here—but that could be some of those heavy metals interfering. I'm afraid that if we go down there, we won't have any assistance from the inhabitants. We'll be on our own."

"*Are* there inhabitants?" Rocket asked. "As in genuine sentients?"

"Yes," Gamora answered, "and what's more, they are building a civilization. There are cities down there, but they haven't yet reached a very sophisticated level. I'd guess that they are at a swords and bows stage, and that they haven't quite gotten to steam power."

"As long as the raw materials are there, they can still be hitting each over the head with rocks for all I care," Rocket said. "Just get me what I need, and we'll be planning our holidays before you know it."

Quill nodded. "I'm setting the course now. At sublight we should be there within the week."

As he punched in the coordinates, Quill couldn't help but notice the other crew members retreating to their own corners of the ship. Whatever tensions were between them had not dissipated with the talk of holidays. The enmity was still present, submerged like jagged rocks beneath the water's surface, and would emerge again.

CHAPTER 2

Even Drax had to admit that the planet they found themselves on was lovely. The climate was just right, not too hot and not too cold. Their landing site was in the middle of unspoiled forest, and the birds that had fallen silent at their intrusion hadn't waited long to start singing again. The sun was bright and a gentle breeze rustled through the leaves.

"Well, this isn't so bad, is it?" Quill asked.

The others just glared at him, and went about the business of setting up the sensors, consisting of three poles made of a dull, black metal crowned with what looked like an inverted umbrella missing the webbing between its spokes. The poles were linked with copper cabling that was lit up with crackling spirals of blue energy that pulsed along its length. Another cable ran from each of the poles to a computer mounted on a portable stand, and at which Gamora stood punching in commands.

"I am going to do another scan and map out the best concentrations of the minerals we need. I'll also see if I can shed some light on that unreadable area."

"The question is, how long will it take to refine crude ore into what we need?" Rocket asked. "I know the ship can do it, but it won't be a quick process." He tapped some figures into the portable computer he was carrying. "You have got to be kidding!"

"What does it say?" Quill asked.

"Best case scenario, eight months," Rocket said. "Worst case . . . three years."

"You mean I could be stuck in the middle of nowhere for three years?" Drax bellowed. "All because this clown couldn't control his base impulses?"

"I resent that," Quill said. "Besides, you were all saying how you wanted a holiday. Look around, this is a lovely place to spend some time in."

"There is a complete lack of casinos here, unless I have suddenly been struck blind," Rocket said. "I wanted a *real* holiday, not some get-close-to-nature, tree-hugging waste of time. Ah . . . no offense, Groot."

"I am Groot."

"This is not acceptable," Drax snapped. "I will not waste my time here. I have revenge to exact."

"It seems that we don't have much of a choice," Gamora said. "And this isn't that bad when it comes to places where I've been stranded."

"All places are bad when you are stranded," Rocket said, "A cage is a cage, even if it is planet sized."

Thinking about some of the stories Rocket had told him about his past, Quill actually started to feel guilty. It was an odd sensation, and one he didn't relish.

"I'm sorry, Rocket," Quill said. "I just don't know what choice we have."

"We could build a beacon," Gamora said suddenly. "We've got all the parts we need."

"We're in the middle of nowhere—uncharted space," Quill said. "Who do you think is going to come get us? Even if they do get the signal, which isn't guaranteed, it's a long way back to known space."

"I don't know, Quill. I think we could pretty easily deal with the distance issue," said Rocket, intrigued now that it was a technical challenge. "We could boost the signal and target that anomaly. It got us here, so it stands to reason it might be two way. What is it going to hurt to try?"

"Exactly," Gamora said enthusiastically. "Encode the hyperspace coordinates, and whoever comes for us can do it the easy way instead of being chewed up and spat out by that thing like we were."

"You're forgetting something," Drax said. Everyone turned to look at him. "There are a lot of people out there with no reason to love us. It could be one of them who comes after us, all guns blazing—or who simply melts the planet down to slag because we are here."

"You're paranoid, Drax," Rocket said, but he didn't sound like he believed it. "I'm not going to stay on this planet just because you're scared of something that might never happen."

"Scared? Are you calling me a coward?"

"Let's not start this again," Gamora said. "I think Drax has a point, but I'm not sure we have a choice. The scan should be done shortly—let's just wait and see what the sensors tell us. Maybe we've missed something—"

She cut off midsentence as the clearing filled with a strange whistling noise that increased in volume with every passing second.

"Take cover!" Drax roared. "That's a missile!"

They looked at each other in horror, and then bolted for the trees. They had just taken cover behind a massive log—the remains of some arboreal giant—when there was a surprisingly small explosion followed by a blinding flash of light. The group thought they were out of the blast range, but suddenly Rocket cursed furiously and inventively.

"Damn it, that hurt," he growled.

Quill glanced over, scared that the raccoonoid had caught a piece of shrapnel or something. Instead, Rocket was looking down at his wrist, where what remained of his wrist comp was a smoking ruin. As they watched, it burst into flame, and Rocket yanked it off, throwing it to the ground and stamping out the fire.

"What the . . . ?" Quill asked, trying make sense of what he had just seen.

"That was an EMP," Rocket said. Drax looked confused. "An electromagnetic pulse," he continued. "Designed to destroy anything electronic."

"The ship!" Quill shouted, horrified.

They sprinted back to the clearing and stopped cold, looking with shock at the scene that confronted them. There was little structural damage, as the blast itself had been fairly contained, but the high-energy pulse had wreaked havoc—the sensors were canted at crazy angles and smoke poured from the computer. Some of the spokes had melted and drooped towards the ground, and the cables had become lines of fire on the grass. This seemed like the least of their problems, however, since more smoke poured from the ship itself. Fortunately, when they opened the hatch—with Drax and Groot lifting the slab of metal by hand—there was no sign of fire. Still, what they found was bad enough. All of the computer systems were dead and refused to power back up. The failsafes had kicked in, and so the high-tech fuses had blown, preventing the complete destruction of the delicate circuitry. Quill had spares, but he expected to need only two or three a year—and there were at least a hundred fuses that needed replacing. He didn't even want to look at the engine room.

"Quill, you should see the engine room," Rocket called out. "It's pretty bad."

Quill sighed; that was the last thing he needed to hear. He started to inventory the rest of the damage. Besides the main computer systems, the EMP had also fried the backups. Then a terrible thought struck him. He hurried to his cabin and pulled a footlocker from underneath the bed.

Aside from the ship itself, the locker was Quill's most expensive possession, and he hoped that it had been worth the credits he hadn't really been able to afford to spend on it. He punched the keypad and heard a whirring noise as the chest unlocked—that was a good sign at least. He lifted the heavy alloy lid with trembling fingers and pulled out his face mask and element gun. Relief washed through him—they looked undamaged and the brief diagnostics he ran confirmed it. The dodgy-looking Flb'Dbi who had sold him the locker had sworn that it would protect against fire, blasts in the two kiloton range, and EMP weapons. Quill had only half-believed him, but was happy to have been proven wrong. His equipment had gotten him out of many tight spots, and been with him so long, that it would have been awful to lose it. He placed the pieces back in the locker, armed the lock, and then slid the chest back under his bed. Everything would be safer there for now, especially with someone—or something—launching missiles at them.

When he returned to the control room, Rocket was elbow deep in the console, with Gamora passing him tools in response to his barked commands. Groot was smiling at nothing in particular, and Drax was leaning sullenly against the wall, his muscular arms crossed in front of him.

"Is it as bad as I think it is?" Quill asked.

"Worse," Rocket replied. "Not only do you lack spares for even a fraction of the parts that need replacing, I'm not even going to know if the subroutines have been wiped until I power the console back up."

"Well, the good news is that I do have a backup of the operating system in a blast-proof locker," Quill replied, "and I think it made it though okay."

"Good news, huh? Well here's the bad news," Rocket countered. "Without the ship's computer, I can't fabricate the parts we need to repair it—and I can't get the ship up and running without those parts. See the problem there? It's a vicious circle."

"I fought in a vicious circle once," Drax said. "Well, that's what the spice cartel called it, anyway."

"Not helpful, Drax," Gamora said. "Just in case I am misunderstanding, Rocket, you're saying we are trapped on this planet indefinitely?"

"Yes, that's exactly what I'm saying. Even if we get the materials we need, I don't know how to go about fabricating some of the components. The only way we're getting out of here is if someone else lands here—and what are the chances of someone being as unlucky as us and hitting that nebula anytime soon?"

Everyone started yelling at once, venting their frustrations. The cacophony went on for a few minutes until Groot ended it by yelling at the top of his voice.

"I am Groot!"

His bellow echoed in the narrow confines of the ship's

control room, and the rest of the group went abruptly silent, ears ringing. Groot just smiled and went back to examining his leaves. When he could hear again, Quill spoke.

"Look, we know there's at least some technology on the planet," he said. "Maybe the inhabitants can help us."

"Yes, because they seem so friendly," Rocket said sarcastically. "We are outgunned. Well, we would be if we *had* some guns. And the longer we sit in one place, the greater the chance of another attack. We need to get moving. Now."

"We should at least investigate the possibility of help from the locals. What have we got to lose?"

"Other than our lives?" Gamora asked.

"Since when has that stopped us?" Quill turned to Drax. "We know *you* don't want to stay here. Don't you think we should go and investigate at least?"

"We? I remember before there was a 'we.' I seemed to be doing much better for myself," Drax said. "I think perhaps it is time for me to try being alone again."

Quill was at a loss for words for a moment.

"You can't be serious. We're a team, and if we're going to get out of here, we need to stick together."

"It was following your lead that got us stranded here," Drax said. "That seems to be a good reason to ignore your suggestions. Besides, all of you have held me back too many times."

"All of us? What's that supposed to mean?" Rocket snapped.

"I've bailed you out more times than I can remember, and so has the big guy."

"I am Groot."

"Drax doesn't need help from a rodent and a walking plant," Drax said.

"Why I oughta . . ."

"Enough!" Gamora yelled. "That's it, I am done. I am sick of your squabbling. I wanted time alone as well, and I am going to take it. You can all do whatever you want, but I will be somewhere far away. Maybe after you've all grown up a bit, I'll go investigating with you, but the truth is that this planet has everything I need—and what I need most is some solitude."

She started towards the exit, only to stop as Quill cut her off.

"Gamora . . ."

"Get out of my way, Quill, or I will go straight through you," she said, danger in her voice. "I haven't forgotten that we wouldn't be here if it weren't for you."

Not wanting to give away how much her words had hurt him, Quill stepped aside without saying anything, and then she was gone. He turned back to the others.

"You guys aren't leaving, too, are you?"

Drax straightened up and walked to the door. "I need time to think and decide my next course of action," he said.

"Don't be stupid, Drax," Quill said. "What are you going to

do out there? Become a woodcutter? All you know is fighting. You need us."

The moment he said it, Quill knew it was a mistake.

Drax drew himself up. "I do not need anyone."

With that he left, not looking back even once.

"Good work, Quill. I don't think that you could have stuffed that up any better if you'd tried," Rocket said. "You know what Drax is like about his stupid honor. Very prickly."

Quill rounded on him furiously.

"*He's* prickly? Pot. Kettle. Black. Couldn't you have been a bit more polite?" Quill asked.

"Hey, don't blame me, Quill. Gamora was right. We wouldn't be in this situation if it weren't for you. Don't take it out on me."

"If you had to deal with this group, you'd be looking for some distraction, too."

"Is that right?" Rocket asked. "Well, I guess you won't need to worry about dealing with us anymore. The others are gone, and I don't really feel like hanging around here, either. C'mon, Groot."

"You don't have to go anywhere, Groot. You can stay here," Quill said.

"I am Groot," he said sadly, moving to stand with Rocket.

"Look, Quill, maybe this is for the best. We can all take some time to regroup and calm down a bit. But if we don't do something, someone is going to say something that can't be taken back, and it will tear the group apart. We've been through too much together for a setback like this to divide us—I think we just need a bit of a break," Rocket said, not unkindly; Quill's despair must have shown on his face and the raccoonoid was trying to console him. "There's no rush—we aren't going anywhere. Come and find us after a while, and then we can take it from there."

Rocket grabbed his backpack. "Good luck, Quill."

He turned and walked to the door. Groot reached out and placed a hand on Quill's shoulder, and Quill felt a wave of calmness wash over him.

"I am a Groot," Groot said in a soft voice, and smiled. Then he followed Rocket, and Quill was alone.

Quill sat in the pilot's chair and buried his face in his hands, wondering what he was going to do now. Then, with an almost physical effort, he shook off his despair and stood up, filled with a new resolve. It was a brand-new planet, after all, and he was going to find himself some adventures.

CHAPTER 3

Three months later . . .

The Duke's daughter definitely didn't take after her father. She gazed back across the table at Quill with eyes of such a dark blue as to seem almost violet in the flickering lights of the vast feasting hall. Long, blonde hair cascaded down her back, but was bound up around her temples with a fine silver mesh studded with sapphires. Her delicate, fine-boned features stood in stark contrast to the Duke's jutting jaw and the bent nose that had been broken in some long-ago battle. All in all, Quill was much happier looking at her.

"So, Lord Quill, tell me about this strange land you come from," she said. "Are all the men skilled warriors, as you are?"

"Well, Karyn . . . if I may call you that, my lady?" Quill had quickly fallen into the archaic and formal speech patterns of the court's nobility. A hundred scams and heists had made him a natural mimic, able to be all things to all people.

At her nod, he continued. "I have had the advantage of traveling to many different places and picking up bits and pieces of their fighting systems. Added up, the variety gives me an edge when it comes to many things."

Karyn nodded, immediately grasping his point. Quill knew that a number of suitors had missed the intelligence beneath the beauty and paid the price, and he resolved that he would not make the same mistake. He had been trying to get to know her better for almost three months, since he had first laid eyes on her, and this was the deepest conversation they'd had in all that time.

"I actually haven't been back to the city where I was born since I was young, so I can't tell you too much about it." He paused, and then continued on in a much quieter voice. "In fact, only one good memory from that place has stayed with me."

Karyn leaned towards him. "And what's that?"

"My mother. The last time I saw her was the night she died."

Karyn's blue eyes softened and she leaned farther forward to take his hand in hers.

"You poor man," she said gently.

Before Quill could say anything more, a crash echoed through the banquet hall as the doors flew open hard enough to bounce off of the walls on either side of the doorway. There, silhouetted in the light streaming through the entrance, was a massive figure. Quill was not a small man, but the newcomer would tower over him side by side, and was at least twice as wide through the shoulders as Quill was.

"Ah, our guest has arrived!"

The Duke's bellow cut through the silence that had descended after the newcomer's dramatic entrance. An older man, but still vigorous, the Duke of Vylara's voice carried the unmistakable air of someone used to having his words listened to and obeyed, and the fifty or so nobles who had gathered to witness the night's proceedings turned their eyes towards him. The banquet hall could have held ten times as many, but much of the nobility had retired to summer estates. Even so, the chamber was still an impressive sight, with tattered banners and other trophies of war hanging on the walls alongside exquisite works of art. The graceful arches of the roof gave it an airy feel, and polished silver lamps threw soft light that created the illusion of the night sky under a full moon. The Duke was himself an imposing figure, clad in rich blue robes of a simple yet obviously expensive cut, and bracelets of beaten gold glimmered at his wrists.

"Will you join us for meat and mead before we settle the matter at hand?" the Duke asked.

"I am here to fight." The newcomer's voice was flat and emotionless. "There will be time for food when your champion has fallen."

Quill flushed with anger at the man's arrogance. With an effort of will, he forced it back down—fighting angry was a sure way to get hurt. If the Duke shared Quill's anger, his voice gave no sign of it.

"So be it. Step forward and take your place, and the ceremony can begin."

Without another word, the newcomer strode past the banquet tables and into an open space that had been cleared in the middle of the hall. As the light fell on his face, it revealed blunt features, all lines and angles—like the man had been carved from rock. Cold eyes glared from beneath brooding eyebrows, and his hair was cut close to his scalp. The man was clad only in tight, leather trousers, his huge torso bare except for the scars and gouges left by countless fights. Quill nodded; this was obviously a seasoned warrior, otherwise he wouldn't be representing an entire duchy. The lack of loose fabric to provide his opponent a grip and the shorn hair to prevent another fighter grabbing it showed that the other man had been through the mill a time or two. Quill knew that he should have shaved his head too, but women liked his thatch of hair too much for him to want to. Instead, he would wear a skullcap made of leather to stop his opponent from taking advantage of his vanity. With a sigh, Quill stood and made his way into the circle, standing beside the other man and trying not to think about the difference in their sizes.

The Duke's voice took on a formal tone as he began to speak, as if the words were not his but were instead weighted with tradition stretching back long before his reign.

"Nobles of Vylara, and our guests, the witnesses for the Duke of Krydor," he began, "for two hundred years we have eschewed wars between us. Instead of the waste of young lives and the watering of battlefields with the precious blood of our people, we have instead chosen a more civilized path to settle our disputes. Today, you will witness two champions doing battle to decide the status of the village of Remore, which both duchies claim. The Duke of Krydor and I have sworn on our honor that we will abide by the result. Do you so witness?"

"*We do so witness.*"

The voices that echoed back strong and clear from the tables were solemn, but Quill could still hear an undercurrent of excitement.

"Good. Now, let our two champions be known. For Vylara stands Lord Quill, a newcomer to our duchy, but a warrior whose skills have elevated him to the rank of my personal champion within a few short months."

There was a pounding of tables as the gathered nobles, the majority of whom were Vylarans, saluted him. Quill tried not to grin. His ascent had been rapid indeed, the result of a duel fought before the Duke when Quill had been challenged by an outraged husband. The man had been skilled enough, but Quill—able to call upon the fighting disciplines of a score of planets—had defeated him easily. The Duke, a shrewd tactician, had seen the potential use for such a fighter immediately, and Quill had since stood in a dozen bouts on the Duke's behalf—winning each one. It was a strange system of diplomacy, but Quill had no complaints, as it had provided him a niche he could happily fill—as well as his own title and comforts. In fairness, it had also allowed him to prevent several potentially fraught situations that the Duchy had faced from blowing up into battles. Of course, the downside was that he had to fight.

"For Krydor," the Duke continued, "stands Ragnak, undefeated in ten battles."

Ragnak raised his massive arms above his head, clenching his huge fists. Quill himself was tall and well built, with broad shoulders tapering to a slim waist and flat stomach, but next to Ragnak he felt like a child. The sheer size of the man was disconcerting, and Quill could only hope that Ragnak was as slow as that bulk of muscle must demand. He was easily the biggest man Quill had seen since he had come to the planet, most of the inhabitants being Quill's height or shorter.

The Duke turned to the other duchy's champion.

"As our guest, custom dictates that you have choice of weapons. What say you?"

Quill relaxed a bit. The local weapon disciplines were relatively unsophisticated, and whether the other man chose blade or staff, Quill was confident his speed and skill would be more than adequate.

"I need no weapon other than my hands." In another man it might have sounded like bravado, but Ragnak spoke with a casual indifference that made Quill's blood go cold.

The Duke blinked in surprise, and then regained his composure.

"So be it." He sat back down in in his seat. "Take your places."

Quill stood and faced the other man, trying to maintain an air of confidence.

"So, old chap, what do you say we make this a fair fight? No biting, gouging, or anything like that? No need to forget our manners."

Ragnak gave no sign of having heard him other than a slight curl of his lip that Quill might have simply imagined.

"All right then, not a big talker. Let's see how you fight."

The Duke's voice rang out across the hall. "Begin!"

The two champions circled each other warily, each waiting for the other to commit. Quill was content to wait and let the bigger man come at him—so Quill could try to use his opponent's bulk and strength against him—but Ragnak seemed in no hurry. Quill began to sweat. Usually men this big were arrogant because of their size, and could be lured into costly errors. If Ragnak was a patient fighter, it would make him twice as dangerous. Quill was just about to feint at the other man when Ragnak exploded into motion, charging at Quill with a speed that was as terrifying as it was unpredictable. The off-worlder was barely able to dodge to one side, ducking under a punch that whistled through the air just above his head. Quill pivoted and drove his fist into the other man's back, aiming for Ragnak's kidneys with short, sharp jabs, but with all the power that he could muster. Three times Quill hit him, wincing as each blow landed. It was like driving his fist into an oaken board, the thick muscle barely yielding beneath each punch. Ragnak showed no sign of pain, instead spinning around and throwing another brutal punch. Caught by surprise, Quill windmilled backwards to get out of reach, but was not quick enough. The Krydoran's huge fist clipped Quill's chin, barely touching him, but the impact was still enough to send bright stars flashing before his eyes. Catching his balance, Quill spat a mouthful of blood on the floor and watched the other champion carefully, waiting for another charge.

It was not long in coming, and Quill braced himself against the onslaught. Ragnak's huge arms lashed out as Quill desperately blocked them. He drove his fist into the inside of Ragnak's elbow, a blow that should have left the other man's limb numb and useless, but that instead nearly broke Quill's wrist. The pain was enough that he barely remembered to throw up his other arm to block another punch. This time he felt the impact all the way to his shoulder, and it was his own arm that felt numb, nerves tingling. He couldn't believe how strong the other man was; it was like sparring with Drax. Of course, Drax usually remembered to pull his punches. Quill had never imagined a mere human could hit this hard. A more subtle approach to combat seemed called for, and Quill stepped inside the next blow, grabbing Ragnak's wrist and using the big man's strength to flip him over his shoulder. Ragnak hit the floor with a crash that shook the hall, and for a moment Quill let himself hope that the other man might stay down. Instead, Ragnak rose fluidly to his feet, the only sign of his fall the wary respect he now showed Quill. Rather than charging straight at the off-worlder, Ragnak now began to stalk him, hands outstretched, clenching and unclenching. Quill moved back, trying to stay outside the Krydoran's reach, uncomfortably aware that if Ragnak got his hands on him, it would be the end.

An uneasy mutter rose from the tables scattered around the hall, caught and magnified by the ornate marble walls. The Vylarans were used to seeing their champion make short work of all comers, and it must have disoriented them to see him struggling in such a fashion. Quill tried to ignore the mutterings, but it was hard not to feel a slight sting at the Vylarans' doubt. He gritted his teeth as he heard a familiar voice among the babble—Karyn asking her father if he thought Quill would prevail. That was too much for Quill, and he launched himself at Ragnak, spinning into a perfect crescent kick that should have shattered the other man's collarbone. Instead, Quill groaned as his ankle was caught in a viselike grip—the Krydoran was fast! With contemptuous ease, Ragnak yanked Quill towards him and caught Quill around the throat, lifting him from the floor before hurling him backwards and crashing down onto one of the tables. For a moment, Quill simply laid atop the wreckage before finally clambering to his feet. He shook off splinters of wood and the ruins of a meal that the luckless noble who had cushioned his fall had been eating. Quill's legs didn't want to obey him, and nearly sent him down to the unforgiving floor, but he was conscious of the Duke's (and more importantly, his daughter's) eyes upon him, and, by sheer willpower, forced his legs to support his weight.

"Okay, Ragnak, I'm done playing with you," Quill said, hoping his voice didn't ring as hollow in everyone else's ears as it did in his own. "We can do this the easy way . . . or the hard way."

For the first time, Ragnak smiled, his grin hard and merciless.

"Oh, the hard way. I insist."

Quill shrugged and waded in, his fist crashing into the Krydoran's chin with all of his strength behind it. This time, the huge champion gave the barest sign of being hurt, wincing and shaking his head slightly, but before Quill could press his advantage, Ragnak came at him. Quill ducked under the first punch and buried his other fist in Ragnak's midriff, but again, it was like hitting a plank of wood, and the Krydoran barely grunted. Quill threw another punch, trying to break the other man's nose, but instead gasped as his fist was caught in one of Ragnak's huge hands. Slowly, the giant began to squeeze, grinding the bones in Quill's hand together. Quill strained against the other man's grip, but he might as well have been fighting one of the bronze statues scattered about the hall. Desperately, he threw another punch with his free hand, driving it into Ragnak's cheekbone, but the other man barely blinked. Quill threw another punch, then another, mashing

Ragnak's lips into his teeth, and all the while the Krydoran merely grinned a bloody smile and squeezed harder. Quill's next punch was too slow and Ragnak caught it in his free hand, leaving Quill trapped—and at his mercy.

"You fought better than I expected when I first saw you," Ragnak said. "You looked like another soft lord who couldn't take a punch. I'll make this quick in honor of your bravery."

Before Quill could say anything, Ragnak yanked him forward. The last thing Quill saw was the other man's forehead hurtling towards his face, and then everything went black.

CHAPTER 4

Quill was used to hangovers, but at least with those there were usually some fond memories of the night before to ease the pain. He didn't even have that to offset the splitting headache that was making him feel like the top of his head could slide off at any time, instead, he had only the humiliating realization that he had been beaten. The night before was nothing more than a blurry memory, but he needed no reminder to tell him what had happened. The glares from the other men gathered around the table in the Duke's personal audience chamber were eloquent enough. As the Duchy's champion, he enjoyed a place on the Duke's council, but even on a good day he normally kept as quiet as possible and let the more established members go about their business. Today, he slouched in his seat and tried to be invisible, hoping this would be a quick meeting and that he could retire to his chambers and lick his wounds sooner rather than later. But instead, he winced as the voices around him grew louder and louder.

"Without the harvest from Remore, there will be a shortage of purple dye this season, and that means less revenue than we had planned for."

That was the Master of Coin, a red-faced man named Tremas in his late sixties who treated every penny that came through the Duchy's coffers as his own—and who squealed like a pig whenever asked to spend any.

"Perhaps you should not have planned for the harvest from a village that was in dispute," said Marius, the Master of Arms. Also in his sixties, he was lean where Tremas was fat, and still one of the best swords in the Duchy. He and Quill had been if not friends, at least on good terms since the off-worlder had taught Marius some of the blade techniques he had learned from Gamora. The thought of Gamora gave Quill a melancholy twinge. Despite the way that they had parted, he often wondered what she, and his other companions, were doing— and whether they were okay. Just as he did every other time they came to mind, he pushed down the memories of their time together and focused on the task at hand. That way led to less time for regret.

There were four other lords in the chamber, all with their own areas of oversight and authority, but Quill had soon learned that it was Marius and Tremas who mattered. The Duke gave more weight to either of their words than he did to the rest of his advisors combined. The two men were very different in attitude and experience but, while Quill tended to side with Marius, he had to admit that their different perspectives meant that the Duke got to see both sides of a problem—and the Duchy was often the better for it.

"If our champion had done his job," said Tremas, "the village would no longer be in dispute." Scorn dripped from his voice, as he had no fondness for Quill. As far as Tremas was concerned, the council was for nobility, not landless strangers whose only distinction was a talent for violence. "Instead, it now belongs to Krydor."

"Every man can be beaten on his day, and Krydor chose well—that champion, Ragnak, was a brute," Marius said. "Or do you think you could have done better?"

Tremas sneered. "It isn't my role to fight. I leave that to those with more brawn than brains."

Despite his resolution to remain silent, Quill was about to attempt a biting comeback when the Duke brought his fist crashing down on the table. The noise sent daggers of pain through Quill's battered skull, and silenced the other men in the room.

"Enough! Quill has won enough bouts to prove his worth. I would have preferred he won, but he didn't. Let that be the end of it." Tremas stirred as if to speak, but the Duke quelled him with a glare. "I said that is the end of it. Given the tidings we have just received, Remore is a trivial matter indeed."

None of the other men argued, instead turning to stare at the nervous young courier who seemed to be trying to fade into the wallpaper. It was the first they'd heard that there was another threat to the Duchy.

"Tell the council your news," the Duke commanded.

"Sire," the youth stammered. "Astarlia has fallen, and its armies are scattered. I barely made it out alive."

Gasps rang out from the gathered lords, and Quill straightened in his seat, forgetting his pain for a moment. Astarlia was the easternmost province of the Empire, standing as a bulwark against the nomadic tribes that wandered the steppes beyond the eastern border. The bulk of the Empire's standing army was stationed there, as wars within its provinces were virtually unknown, and skirmishes with the nomads were the only battles that had been fought for centuries. If Astarlia had fallen, something had gone terribly wrong—and worse, the rest of the Empire was now vulnerable to the nomads' incursion.

"How is this possible?" Marius asked. The old soldier had a knack for cutting straight to the important questions. "The nomads are formidable warriors one on one, but as an army they lack organization. I can't believe that they could defeat the force we had based on the border."

"My lord," began the courier after gulping nervously, "it was the nomads, but some of the veterans said they'd never seen them move in such numbers. We've held our own against them before, but they were organized this time. They didn't just charge at us, they fought like, well, like soldiers. And they had better weapons than we'd seen before. Strange, flat-looking bows with ranges like ours, but that could shoot four or five times as fast, and proper armor like our knights wear—but all their soldiers had it. It didn't even seem to slow them down, and they were riding steppe ponies, not knights' coursers." He stopped for a moment, as if looking at something only he could see. "But, that wasn't what broke us, my lord."

"Go on," the Duke said with surprising gentleness. "What was it?"

"It was these dark figures, sire, like shadows that walked and moved on their own, or rode horses as black as night with eyes that glowed with a blood-red light. They directed the nomads, urged them on. And every time we tried to make a stand, they would be at the head of the charge and we just couldn't hold against them. They had swords of fire that sliced through steel like butter, and they could take blows that would have killed a normal man without even blinking!"

"This is ridiculous," Tremas sputtered. "You expect to us to believe these . . . these fairy tales? They sound like an attempt to cover up cowardice."

"But they're not fairy tales, my lord," the courier protested. "You have to believe me. We fought as hard as we could but . . . but, those things . . ." He seemed on the verge of tears, and the Duke raised a hand in a calming gesture.

"It's all right, son. You are not the only courier who made it through." He turned to Tremas and glared at him. "Go easy on him, Tremas. He must have fought his way through the enemy to get here and give us this vital news. Hardly the act of a coward, and he deserves better than your scorn. The other couriers back up his story."

"Thank you, sire," the courier said gratefully.

Tremas nodded grudgingly. "I beg your pardon, lad. You've shown yourself as brave as any man, if not braver. You've served the Duchy well."

The courier flushed and stammered his thanks.

"That was well said, Tremas," Marius seconded.

Quill agreed. Whatever Tremas's faults, he was fair, and, it seemed, capable of being gracious.

The Duke pulled a pouch from his belt. It clinked with the sound of heavy gold coins as he passed it to the courier.

"You may leave us now. Go to the barracks and you will be taken care of. You have our gratitude."

The courier bowed his head in thanks, and half walked, half stumbled from the room.

"Sire, this is deeply disturbing news," Marius said. "Our most experienced warriors were in Astarlia, and if they have fallen, what is there to stop the nomads from ranging deeper into the Empire? And these strange reports . . . even without these new weapons, if something has organized them—whether these dark figures or something else—we will be hard pressed to stand against them."

"Does the Emperor know?" Tremas asked.

The Duke sighed, and for the first time in Quill's experience, looked his true age.

"The Emperor is still a boy, and his regent is no general. I don't think that we can look to the court for help; it will be a long time coming."

Marius nodded, as did Tremas, although more reluctantly. The other men in the room followed suit.

"Then we must do what we can with what we have," Marius said. "We have some troops here, but will you give the order to raise levies, sire?"

"The heralds are already going out to every town between here and what was Astarlia," the Duke said. "My plan is to set out now and gather the levies along the way. We cannot let the nomads establish themselves, or we will never be rid of them."

The rest of the meeting was spent discussing logistics and on planning, but the huge maps that were unrolled and placed on the table made no sense to Quill, while the other men threw around names of towns and roads with easy familiarity. Tremas had a remarkable knack for being able to rattle off facts and figures about even the tiniest of villages, right down to details like the number of men of soldiering age, or the number of spears and shields stored in its warehouse. Quill supposed this skill made Tremas the right man for his job, but the level of detail would have bored Quill to tears even if his head hadn't been pounding like a drum. When the meeting finally came to an end, Quill would have liked nothing more than to go and lie down in a dark room, but instead he simply sat and waited as the other men filed out.

"Yes, Lord Quill?" the Duke asked. Quill could tell from his tone that, despite his earlier comments, the Duke was far from happy with his failure against Ragnak the night before.

"Sire, if we are to defeat this enemy, we need to know more about them. It doesn't sound as if these nomads are behaving the way you've come to expect."

"I am aware of that, Quill. I have sent scouts to try and ascertain their numbers, and to discover whatever else they can."

"No disrespect to your scouts, sire, but I have a great deal of experience in reconnaissance, military intelligence, and infiltration," Quill said. "Let me see what *I* can discover."

The Duke shook his head.

"No, I need my champion with me. You may not have basked in glory last night, but it is your duty to stand beside me if we go to war."

"Sire, one man very rarely makes a difference in a large-scale battle, but in the right place, he can be of much more use. And unless something goes wrong, I will rejoin you before you reach the border. I can move much faster than an army on the march. If I can bring you news of the enemy or even a weakness for you to exploit . . . well, isn't that worth the risk?"

Quill could see that the Duke was tempted, and he pressed his advantage.

"Besides, sire, I may be able to recruit some help that might make more of a difference than I can make alone."

Now he had the Duke's full attention. The other man leaned forward, interest lighting up his eyes.

"What do you mean? What sort of help?"

"Sire, you know that I am not from this continent?"

The Duke nodded. The Empire was at a technological stage roughly analogous to medieval Europe, and they had an understanding of the size of the planet and their place on it. They had, without any hesitation, accepted Quill's story of a long ocean voyage and a terrible shipwreck that had left him stranded.

"Well, I wasn't marooned here alone," Quill went on. "I had friends with me. We had a falling out and went our separate ways, but maybe it's time I tried to patch things up."

"These friends of yours, can they fight as well as you?"

Quill grinned. "Oh, they all have significant talents in that area. If I can convince them to help me, the nomads won't know what hit them. One of them is the best tactician I've ever met, another is the most skilled hand-to-hand fighter I know, and a third is called 'The Destroyer'—and it isn't one of those ironic nicknames." Quill decided against trying to explain Groot. "Let me go and find them to scout out your enemy. The worst case is you lose the champion—one who lost his last bout—and the best case is that you might gain several more warriors who might just make all the difference."

"When can you leave?" When the Duke made a decision, he didn't mess around.

"Tomorrow." Quill promised, realizing that left enough time for one memorable night.

The Duke nodded. "Just remember, I won't be waiting for

you. We will be at the border thirty days from tomorrow—whether you are with us or not. I begrudge the nomads every hour they spend on the Empire's soil."

Quill grinned at him. "I won't keep you waiting, sire."

"Good enough," the Duke said. "And, I can promise you this. If you deliver, gold will never be a problem for you again. I take good care of those who serve me well."

That wasn't what Quill was worried about. He had no doubt that he would be taken care of if he succeeded, but the Duke was a good leader, and part of that was knowing that some things didn't have to be said. Quill knew that if he failed the Duke again, he would soon be looking for another profession. The Duke met his gaze and smiled slightly, as if reading Quill's thoughts.

"Go and make your preparations to leave. If all goes well, I will see you at the border in thirty days."

The Duke's unspoken words hung in the air. One way or another, if things didn't go according to plan, the Duke did not expect to see Quill again.

The woodcutter makes his way deeper into the forest, trying to ignore the eerie silence that has fallen over the woods. No birds sing, nothing moves through the trees, and for a man who has spent all his life in the forest, it feels terribly wrong. He knew that when he stepped over the boundary and entered the territory that the Duke's laws had forbidden them, that there would be no going back, but this is unnatural.

The woodcutter is a huge man, arms corded with muscle and with a bushy red beard cascading down his broad chest. The massive axe slung over his shoulder looks like a toy. But he is dwarfed by the ancient trees that loom over him, leaning in threateningly, as if to devour him.

But he is no coward. He is here because wood has become scarce in the land in which he is entitled to work, and he has a family to feed. He refuses to go home empty handed, to a wife who would never voice her disappointment, to a son and daughter who won't understand why they are going hungry.

He moves towards a copse of likely looking trees and unlimbers his axe. As he works through a few practice swings, he hears a rustling in the branches above him, but he ignores it, comforted to hear some sign of life in the otherwise dead woods.

With a fluid motion, he sends the axe whistling towards the trunk of the tree he has chosen. He gasps in shock as it simply stops, shivering in the air, vibrations traveling along the haft and sending pain shooting through his hands.

His incredulous gaze follows the handle to where it is trapped in a branch-like hand, and then up to a face set into a bark-covered trunk with wide eyes that give it a quizzical, almost friendly look. A shadow detaches itself from the branches above and lands at his feet, sharp fangs bared in a rictus-like grin.

"You've picked the wrong place to be chopping down trees, my friend."

The woodcutter knows that if by some chance he makes it home, he will never break the Duke's law again—but right now home seems a long way away.

CHAPTER 5

Quill slouched sullenly as he rode, muttering under his breath every time the pillion of his saddle dug painfully into him. It was a long time since he had sat on a horse, and even though he had picked the mildest beast he could find, he was still out of his comfort zone. The horse seemed to care little for his unease, and simply kept moving at a mile-eating pace. Occasionally, Quill would dismount to let the horse stop for a few mouthfuls of grass; after all, it wasn't the horse that was causing his foul mood.

After he had left the Duke, everything had seemed to be going wonderfully. Karyn must have heard from her father that Quill had volunteered for an important mission, because she had come to his chamber to check on his wounds from the fight. She had been all sympathy and consideration, and had stayed longer than she had perhaps been expecting. By the time she had left for the night, Quill felt much better about things, and his headache had virtually disappeared. He spent the following hours saying goodbye to some of the many friends he had made around the castle, some of whom had been quite upset to hear he was leaving, and so had insisted on some very thorough leave-takings.

Quill had been in a very good mood while packing his

saddlebags, and had been hoping for a nice, leisurely depar-ture—but suddenly a commotion had penetrated the musty quiet of the stables. He could hear raised voices, and what sounded like an attack on the keep. Drawing his sword, he had rushed into the courtyard, only to come to a sudden stop at the sight of a number of young women hurling abuse (and other, more tangible items) at one another. His stomach had lurched as he recognized some of his friends among the serv-ing girls and—to his horror—Karyn. From what they were yelling, he realized that they'd all had the idea to come and say a final goodbye, not expecting to meet anyone else on the same errand. He'd turned to sidle back into the stables unnoticed, but it was too late. One of the girls had noticed him, and their argument with each other had come to an end as they found a better target for their anger.

Quill shuddered as he remembered his undignified dash for the stables, and the mocking laughter of the stable hands as he had galloped out of the gate. He tried to put it out of his mind as he surveyed the scenery around him. It had taken him only an hour or so to leave the city behind, and as he had moved farther out, shops and bullrings had given way to small, neatly-kept tenant farms. He'd spent the night at one of them, grateful for a final night in a bed, even if it was stuffed with straw instead of feathers, and happy to aug-ment his meager provisions. As the farms grew more spaced out, he saw more and more trees, solitary sentinels becoming copses until, finally, he entered the vast Greenmyre Forest. The road on which he had traveled had gone from a raised thoroughfare wide enough for three wagons to travel comfortably alongside each other to a track rutted with the wheels of woodcutters' carts.

As he pushed deeper into the forest, some sunlight still filtered down through the branches and leaves above his head, but it was definitely dimmer than it had been when he had first entered, and it was still only early afternoon. From all the tales he had heard, it would only get darker, the trees growing closer together and the canopy becoming thicker with each passing mile. Quill sighed and pulled his map from his saddlebag. He had no idea how deep he would have to go, as he was only guessing at his destination. From the moment he had established himself at the castle, he had spent what spare time he had (between fighting and feasting and frolicking) gathering whatever tall tales and rumors came through the court, and trying to glean news of his friends. None of them exactly blended in, but all he had to show for his time was the map in his hands and a rough recollection of the direction in which he had last seen them heading.

Since Quill had entered the forest he'd noticed the signs that woodcutters had been at work. Every mile or so, a shallower set of ruts would diverge from the main road and branch out into the woods, surrounded by stumps where vast trees had been felled and cut into more manageable pieces. The remains of campfires were scattered about, and very occasionally, he would spy a broken tool that had been left to rust—though most woodcutters were far too frugal to waste anything.

And then suddenly everything changed. It was as if he had crossed an invisible line. There were no more stumps, no more ashes of fires past, no more tools scattered around. Even the ruts in the road came to an abrupt end as the road narrowed to a faint track through the forest.

Quill's skin prickled—he had heard about this, but thought that the stories were exaggerated. The Duke's law was clear—on pain of death there was to be no logging past the three-mile boundary, but Quill would have expected there to be a slight blurring of the law. He knew better than anyone that where there was money to be made by bending the rules there would be men willing to do so. But the tales he had heard implied that death by the executioner's axe was a merciful end for those who violated this ancient custom, that those the Duke's soldiers didn't capture met terrible and cruel ends in the forest. Quill had heard that traveling in the forest could be made safer if you harmed no animal and broke no living branch. While he didn't put much stock in fairy tales, he felt it was better to be safe than sorry. Quill didn't even intend to build a fire, and he had enough provisions to see him through without resorting to hunting.

He kept moving through the rest of the day, letting the horse set the pace and allowing it to graze from time to time—

making sure it ate only grass. Quill's eyes gradually adjusted to the changing light, but after a few hours, what light there was became so dim that details faded into shadow only ten or twenty feet ahead. The horse seemed fine following the trail, so Quill continued on until it was so dark that he was convinced that the sun must be setting. Coming into a clearing, he dismounted and gathered a pile of dead wood that he placed in the middle of the clearing. His resolution to avoid a fire had faded with the light, but he still made sure that no overhanging branches could possibly be singed.

After hammering a stake into the ground and securing his mount so it couldn't wander off and get into trouble, Quill laid down next to the fire. The ground, deeply covered with fallen leaves, was more than soft enough to sleep on, and a saddlebag served suitably as a pillow. After the indolent months he had spent in the luxury of the castle, this was actually a refreshing change—and before he knew it, sleep claimed him.

Quill awoke to a rusty axe blade against his throat. Slowly, taking care not to startle the roughly dressed man kneeling above him, Quill opened his hands to show they were empty.

"Let's not do anything hasty here," he said in a soothing voice. "I don't have much gold on me, but you are welcome to take it. I won't come after you, just let me go on my way."

There was low laughter to Quill's right, and he tried to turn towards its source, wincing as the blade's jagged edge nicked his skin. He could make out a group of three or four men—it was hard to make an exact count out of the corner of his eye.

"That's mighty generous of you, my lord." The voice was dripping with sarcasm, and it made "lord" sound like a swear word. "Giving us your permission is very gracious."

"I aim to please," Quill said, keeping his tone light. "Whom do I have the honor of addressing?"

This brought another burst of coarse laughter, and Quill heard footsteps rustling towards him through the leafy cover. A massive figure loomed over him, and rough hands patted him down, pulling the dagger from his boot and taking the sheathed sword that Quill had left lying within easy reach beside him.

"Edric, you can let him up, but stay on your toes," the man said. "This one has a stabby look about him that I don't like."

"Yes, Barak."

Quill was pulled to his feet, and gave a show of brushing himself off, as if more concerned with his appearance than being surrounded by threatening men with wood axes. The knowing smile on Barak's face hinted that perhaps Quill wasn't fooling anyone.

"As you may have realized, I am Barak. Over there are Tomas and Davak, and I believe you have met Edric here."

The man's voiced dripped with mockery as he made the introductions, his formal manner an over-the-top imitation of the Duke's court. His companions grinned in appreciation as Barak gave a florid bow to complete the image.

All the men were wearing homespun clothing and leather boots. The similarity didn't stop there, though, as all were big men with the muscle of those who worked hard day in and day out, swinging axes and dragging logs heavier than they were. Barak was the biggest of the men, but there was a cunning look in his eyes that made Quill think that he was not simply leader by virtue of brawn.

"Tie him up, Edric," Barak commanded.

The other woodcutter pulled Quill's hands roughly behind him and bound them at the wrists tightly enough to hurt, the rough hempen rope scraping his skin.

"So, what happens now, Barak?" Quill asked. "Is there any ending here that sees us all part as friends? The Duke will pay a fine ransom for me."

Quill wasn't actually sure that was true.

"If you are the same young lord who left one step ahead of a furious duke's daughter, then I don't think we will get much of a ransom."

Quill tried not to let his dismay show on his face.

"I have no idea what you're talking about."

Barak just laughed.

"Even if that were so, where would you tell them we captured you? There is no amnesty for men like us. Once you've done what we have, the Duke's men will never rest until they've taken our heads."

"What do you . . ." Quill started to ask, then stopped as he realized that the axes the men held were covered in sap.

"You've been cutting wood here," Quill said.

"Of course we have," Barak replied. "We're woodcutters, and we have a living to make."

"But, the laws . . . the stories of a curse."

Barak spat on the ground in front of him.

"*That* is for the Duke and his laws. What right does the Duke have to sit in his castle and tell me where I can and can't cut wood? His children don't go hungry if he doesn't bring home enough food."

"And the curse?"

"There is no curse," Barak said. "It's a story they tell to scare away the cutters that the Duke's men can't stop. I know dozens of men who have been poaching from the deep forest all their lives, and none of them have been claimed by the curse."

"What about Robar?" Davak asked suddenly. "And Vatar? If you'd asked me a year ago about the curse I would have agreed with you, but a lot of men have disappeared in the last few months."

"Don't be an idiot," Barak snarled. "I told you, the Duke's men likely caught them but disposed of them quietly so people would start talking about the curse again. Or do you want to debate it with me in front of a stranger?"

Barak clenched a huge fist and his knuckles popped with an ominous cracking. The other men muttered among themselves, but none seemed inclined to argue.

"That's better," Barak said. "Anyway, we've taken plenty of wood, so if the curse is real, we're doomed anyway. But if we let this lordling go, or try and ransom him, we won't have to worry about forest demons—it's the Duke who will have our heads on pikes."

There was a sudden rustling in the branches directly above Quill and something moved in the trees around them, circling them. The other men flinched, their eyes darting about the clearing.

"What was that?" Tomas asked, his voice cracking with the beginnings of panic.

"Just a tree cat, or a bird," Barak snapped. "Get a hold of yourself. Edric, kill him. We've ascertained he has nothing of consequence."

Edric hesitated.

"Now," Barak snapped.

Edric stepped forward and raised his axe. Quill tensed, ready to launch himself forward the moment Edric attacked. He was determined to at least go down fighting. Edric took another step, and then fell back, terror in his eyes as a huge shape stepped from the trees. Before the other men could react, a smaller shape dropped in the middle of them, spitting and snarling as it lashed out with claws and teeth.

Quill took advantage of the men's distraction and rammed into Edric, driving his shoulder into the man's midriff. The woodcutter folded up around the blow, his breath leaving with a startled whoosh, the axe flying from his hands. Quill dived for it, landing clumsily on his side and grabbing at the blade with his bound hands. He swore as he cut himself, but then the rope found the axe's edge. A moment's sawing and the thin rope began to part, and then snapped as he pulled hard against the strands. A second later, he was on his knees, bringing the axe up and preparing to raise himself to his feet. He froze, eyeball to eyeball with a pair of insanely gleaming eyes.

"You!"

CHAPTER 6

Rocket didn't seem that happy to see him. Quill knew that the raccoonoid had a hair-trigger temper, but was still surprised when Rocket swung the cudgel he was carrying at his head. Quill ducked beneath the wild swing, only to hear a grunt behind him. When he whirled around, it was to see Barak shaking his hand in pain.

"You can thank me later," Rocket snarled. "Just deal with him."

Without another word Rocket bounded off towards the larger shape, who was now being assailed by the other three woodcutters, their axes swinging in a workmanlike rhythm. An anguished cry echoed across the clearing.

"I am Groot!"

Distracted, Quill only just managed to block Barak's first blow with his axe, sparks cascading from the point of impact as the two blades clashed. The two men circled each other, neither willing to commit too early. Quill's blade instructor had told him that an axe was one of the few weapons where offense truly was the best form of defense, and that when fighting a swordsman, his best chance would be to create an arc of death that his opponent would be terrified to come within. But he had also warned Quill that when two axemen opposed each other, all bets were off.

Barak handled his weapon with a causal competence, holding it as if it were part of him. The axes he and his men used were not battle axes, but were still razor sharp, designed for felling trees and cutting across the grain, rather than splitting logs. The shaft was almost three feet long, and there was only one side to the head, a long curved bit that gleamed wickedly in the light of the setting sun. Quill could hear that the fight behind him was still going on, but he dared not look.

Barak let out a hoarse shout and charged him. The woodcutter spun the axe shaft in both hands, using the momentum of the axe head to bring it up over his head and then down in a whistling arc, driving straight for Quill's head. Quill managed to bring the shaft of his own weapon up in a horizontal block, catching Barak's just beneath the axe head, the shock of the impact sending it rebounding away. Barak stumbled back and Quill pressed his advantage, swinging his axe in a sideways motion. Barak twisted away, but Quill's weapon slashed through the woodsman's tunic, leaving blood trickling down his side.

"Not bad for a soft lordling," Barak said. "I was right, you are dangerous."

With a wordless roar, Barak began to hack at Quill as if he were a tree. Each swing was perfectly placed, economical in motion, but with frightening power behind it. Quill dodged some of the blows and blocked others with desperate parries, but he knew that only one of those attacks needed to strike home—and that that would be the end of the fight. He remembered his instructor's final piece of advice, a last resort when faced with a fighter whose skill matched his own. With a deep breath Quill stepped inside the next swing, grunting as he took the full force of the axe shaft in his side, then brought his knee up between the other man's legs. Barak's eyes widened, and then rolled back in his head as he slid to the ground.

"Ouch," a voice said. Quill spun, raising his axe, then relaxed as he realized it was Rocket behind him. "Talk about a low blow. Effective, though."

"Good to see you, too, Rocket," Quill said. "Are you okay? And the big guy?"

Groot moved up beside Rocket. Behind him the other woodcutters lay in a battered pile.

"I am Groot."

Quill looked at Rocket.

"Yeah, I'm fine, too—thanks for asking."

Groot actually looked a bit worse for wear—a number of gashes in his thick, bark-like skin leaked a sap-like fluid, but as Quill watched, they were already healing.

"Saved your ass again, huh, Star-Lord?" Rocket said sarcastically.

Quill flushed. "I had things under control."

"Yeah, right," Rocket said. "So, what brings you here, anyway?"

Quill grinned at him. "Can't I just pop by to see old friends?"

"I am Groot."

"I agree, buddy, that sounds like a load of manure to me, too," Rocket said. "Just tell us why you're here, Quill. Can we fix the ship?"

As Quill explained the mission he had been given by the Duke, he tried to gauge the reaction of the odd couple before him. Groot was as inscrutable as always. In fact, Quill could never be sure whether the gentle giant was even listening. At that moment, he seemed enraptured by a caterpillar that was winding itself around one of his branches, a broad grin splitting his face. Rocket seemed impassive, but Quill noticed that the raccoonoid's ears were cocked forward and quivering. Maybe their life in the woods wasn't as exciting as Rocket had hoped.

"What are you two doing here in the middle of nowhere?" he asked. "Are you the curse that everyone is talking about?"

Rocket sneered. "The middle of nowhere is right—I've been going out of my mind here. It's incredibly boring and it's not like I get much conversation. Isn't that right, Groot?"

"I am Groot."

"When we left you and the others, we wandered for a little while until we reached the forest. The big guy loved it and he wanted to stay for a while. It's not like I had anywhere else in mind, so we stayed. I listened around a few campfires and heard the stories of the curse, and we decided to use it to our advantage. I'm all for sustainable use of natural resources, but some of these trees have been here for centuries, and there's plenty of wood for them closer to home."

"So what will you do with them?" Quill gestured to the unconscious woodcutters. "Killing in cold blood isn't your usual style."

"I am Groot!"

"Exactly, big guy. We'll leave them on the road and let the Duke decide what to do with them. We aren't judges . . . or executioners."

"Aren't you still just sending them to their deaths?" Quill asked. "The penalty for chopping wood here is the headsman's block."

"It's not our decision, Quill. What would you have us do, just let them go? We might run into them again."

"I've heard of the laws, but why would the Duke be so interested in protecting the forest?" Quill asked. "No one was able to tell me anything about it."

Rocket gestured to the trees.

"Because of them, of course. Why do you think Groot loves it here so much? I may not get much conversation, but he sure as hell does—they haven't stopped nattering away since we got here. They told me about the agreement that they reached with the Duchy generations ago."

Quill's jaw dropped. "The Duchy signed a treaty with . . . trees?"

"Yeah, they're sentient, at least the ones on this side of the boundary. The rest are just normal trees," Rocket said. "They used to be far less . . . treelike, almost humanoid, and that's when the treaty was signed. But that was so long ago, no one in the Duchy remembers them. All they know is that there's a treaty that their forefathers signed, and when it's broken, bad things happen."

Quill felt slightly sick. "So, when they chop down one of these trees . . ."

"Yeah." Rocket's voice was grim. "Apparently they scream for hours."

"I am Groot," Groot said sadly.

"Now do you feel bad about handing them over to the Duke's men?"

"Nowhere near as bad as I did, anyway," Quill replied.

"Good—so we can leave them by the road as planned. I prefer to let other people's problems stay that way. Which is why I don't see why we should tag along with you in the service of some duke."

"Look," said Quill. "I know things got a bit . . . tense back when we landed here. But we've all had time to cool off, and it would be just like old times. Impossible odds, crazy plans—and plenty of gold at the end. What could be more fun?"

"I won't lie, I am bored to tears here," Rocket said. "But it doesn't fix the ship, and I doubt that the big guy is going to be willing leave the forest to fend for itself."

"I am Groot."

"See?" Rocket asked. "He isn't keen."

Quill walked over to Groot and tilted his head back so he could stare into the creature's surprisingly expressive eyes.

"Groot, I do understand why you would want to stay here. You've done a wonderful job protecting these trees; you should be very proud of yourself," he said gently. "But the invading nomads aren't just killing people—they're also chopping down every tree that they come across just to fuel their war machine."

"I am Groot."

Did Quill detect a slight quivering in his voice? He wasn't sure, but he went on.

"What do you think they'll do when they get here? Do you think they'll know that some of these trees are sentient, or even if they do—that they'll care?" he asked. "We're the only chance of stopping them. We need to find out who is helping the nomads, and we need to get that information to the Duke so he has a chance against them. I need you, Groot. You aren't abandoning your friends here—you're just protecting them somewhere else."

"I am Groot," Groot said sadly.

"I guess we're both coming with you," Rocket said.

Groot strode from the clearing, stopping to stand in the middle of a closely bunched group of trees. He was humming, a deep note that seemed to vibrate through air and into Quill's bones. The giant raised his arms above him, reaching towards the sky, tendrils waving back and forth as he swayed gently. As Rocket and Quill watched, flowers sprouted from the tips of Groot's fingers, a rainbow of different colored blooms. A sweet perfume drifted towards them, and Quill felt his eyes prickle with tears as he recognized the scent his mother used to wear. Beside him, Rocket was sobbing as if caught in his own memories, and Quill wondered what his companion was thinking of.

Groot's humming rose in pitch and volume, and he brought his arms down, plunging them into the rich soil at his feet. Cords of muscle-like fibers bunched and flexed under his rough, bark-like skin, as if he were wrestling with the ground, which Quill could have sworn he felt quivering under his feet. There was a sudden burst of rustling behind them, and they turned to see trees writhing and shifting in a line as far as the eye could see into the gathering twilight. As they stared in wonder, the trees seemed to reach towards their neighbors, branches weaving together to form a solid wall twice as tall as Groot.

The wall continued to thicken, bolstered by thorns and spikes. Quill wouldn't have wanted to try and climb it, even less so when he saw tendrils of poison ivy wind their way around the branches. It was a formidable barrier, and Quill guessed that its sudden appearance would feed a hundred tales of curses, and be almost as much protection as the wall itself.

Groot's humming came to an abrupt end, and he staggered momentarily before pulling his arms from the ground. As he rejoined them, Quill shook his head—every time he thought he had lost the ability to be amazed by the giant, he was shown the error of his ways. This was only the latest in a long line of marvels.

"I am Groot." Groot sounded wearier than Quill had ever heard him.

"Are you okay? That was incredible, but . . . did it hurt?"

"I am Groot."

"He'll be all right," said Rocket. "Won't you, big fella?"

"I am Groot."

Without another word, Groot picked up the woodcutters, effortlessly lifting all four. He carried them to the barrier, not even slowing down as he approached, but before he could crash into them, the branches parted before him. Groot stepped through and gently placed the men on the ground, then stepped back through. The wall closed seamlessly behind him, leaving no trace behind of the opening.

"Which way are we going?" Rocket asked, wasting no time.

Quill went through his saddlebags and pulled out the map. He pointed away from the barrier, deeper into the forest.

"West."

"But the only thing that way is the mountains," Rocket said. "Oh, won't *that* be fun."

"Of course it will be—we always have fun," Quill said. "If you're a good raccoonoid, I'll teach you how to ski."

Rocket bared his teeth. "Don't patronize me. Just lead the way."

"Good enough," Quill said. "We have a long way to go, and I'm on a schedule."

He started walking west, and smiled. They did have a long way to go, but having two of his friends back by his side filled him with a renewed sense of hope.

The young girl huddles in the shadow of the ruined stable, back pressed into the corner where two crumbling walls come together. She shivers, arms clasped around slim legs, the smell of smoke harsh in the air. Mixed with the scent of wood smoke is something else, a sickly-sweet smell that reminds her of the rare times when the elders call a feast and slaughter a pig to roast over an open fire.

She chokes back a sob and tries to ignore the sound of clashing blades and pitiful screams, hoping that if she pretends enough they will simply go away. As hours pass, they do fade, an eerie silence falling over the night. The moon is full, illuminating the ground around her, sending strange shadows reaching towards her.

As she watches in terror, the shadows resolve into the men that have sent her fleeing into the night. The swords they hold before them are stained with blood, and one of them has a smudge of ash across his cheek. Their faces are almost bestial with the emotions playing across them. Anger. Excitement. Lust.

As they move towards her, she presses back against the rough brick of the walls. She is trapped, nowhere to go, and all she can do is watch them draw closer. There is a blur of motion, and a figure leaps from the darkness, springing over their heads and landing in a crouch between them and the girl.

Slowly the figure straightens, and the men relax as the moonlight reveals the figure of a beautiful woman, her skin a strange color in the silvery light. She looks somehow fey, fragile, overshadowed by the brutish menace of the men surrounding her.

The girl's heart sinks; what she thought was rescue is merely another victim. One of the men laughs.

"Tonight is our lucky night, boys."

They begin to skulk towards her, and the girl sees the newcomer tense and then—faster than the eye can see—there are two blades in her hands, glimmering viciously in the moonlight.

"You're wrong," the woman says. "Tonight is about to become the worst night of your life."

What follows will stay with the girl for the rest of her life, violent poetry that will shape everything she does.

CHAPTER 7

"**S**o, do you really think you'll find her there?" Rocket asked. "There *are* other women warriors in the world, you know. It's not like they have a club."

Quill scowled at the raccoonoid. They had been walking for days, and his boots—while the height of court fashion—were a cavalryman's show, and not designed for walking. He was sore and tired and grumpy, and they'd had this conversation more than once.

"Rocket, as I keep telling you, I don't really know," he said, trying to stay patient. "The only clue I have is from the interrogation of a bandit the Duke captured. He was half mad and he kept rambling about a raid on a mountain village that went wrong when some mysterious woman decimated their party. It's not much to go on—but the way he described her did sound like Gamora. I can't imagine her staying completely out of trouble, can you?"

"I am Groot."

"Yeah, that's right. She probably would have stabbed at least one idiot by this point," Rocket said. "I still don't know how she hasn't put a blade in you by now, the way you moon over her."

Quill flushed. "I'm sure I don't know what you mean. And

maybe you should save your breath—we'll hit the mountains soon."

Ahead of them, rocky slopes climbed from the trees, looming over the forest as they rose to towering peaks. Far above them, Quill could make out the white gleam of snow on the higher peaks, but the cliffs below them were barren and rocky. As the travelers pushed on, the forest began to thin and the ground became dotted with huge boulders, refugees from some cataclysmic avalanche that Quill hoped was now a part of ancient history. The leaf-covered ground below them slowly gave way to bare stone, and by late afternoon they had left the forest completely behind them. The trail they followed began to twist and turn, following the lay of the land rather than forging its own path—and even Rocket spent long stretches in silence as it grew steeper and steeper.

But it was Quill who suffered most. His boots had little grip and he was constantly slipping and sliding, the extra effort required to keep moving forward taking its toll after months of feasting and roistering. Despite his bulk, Groot made much easier going of things, his rootlike toes digging into the ground with each step, finding cracks in the stone and wedging themselves in, giving him perfect purchase as he stolidly put one foot after the other.

Meanwhile, Rocket could have been designed for this trail, his light weight and prehensile toes letting him climb with ease. He would scout ahead and then bound back down the trail, grinning mockingly at Quill as he raced around his companions.

"Nothing ahead but more climbing, Quill," he shouted. "Isn't this fun?"

Quill gritted his teeth as the raccoonoid dissolved into fits of laughter.

"Yeah, couldn't think of anything I'd rather be doing right now. No sign of any monks?" He paused. "Of anything, for that matter?"

"Nothing. Not even a mountain goat."

Quill frowned. "It's strange. I hate to sound like a cliché, but it's too quiet. I feel like we're being watched."

Rocket lifted his head and sniffed at the air.

"I can't smell anyone nearby, but it's hard to tell," he said. "This rock doesn't hold a scent very well, and there isn't any wind at all."

"I guess we just keep climbing then," Quill said.

He tried not to let his worry show. Time was ticking by, and he was terribly conscious of each day that had passed. It looked like they would be spending at least one night in the mountains. And even if they found Gamora and convinced her to come with them, there was another long journey ahead of them.

The path narrowed as it passed between two peaks, to the point where they had to walk single file. But as it emerged from between the cliffs, the path suddenly widened out into a bowl-shaped valley surrounded by vertical walls of stone. The tops of the cliffs were covered with broken pieces of stone, creating natural ramparts and making it impossible to discern what, if anything, might be up there. It made Quill uneasy, and his skin crawled as they walked into the center of the rocky hollow. It was a terribly exposed position, and Quill tried not to think of the carnage even one skilled archer could wreak from such a strong vantage point. You could bring an army into passes like this and come out with nothing but mincemeat. But there was no army here—only the three of them. He hoped there was nothing waiting in the mountains that might see them as enemies.

"This is a killing ground if I ever saw one," Rocket said. "I hope these monks, if they exist, are friendly."

"Thanks for that," Quill snapped. "Very reassuring. Just what I wanted to hear."

"Sorry," the raccoonoid muttered. "Just making conversation."

They made their way to the other side of the basin without incident, and followed the path into another valley. This one was shallower, but much broader and far less exposed. The floor of the pass was covered with boulders, many so weathered by wind and water that they had taken on the appearance of massive columns. Anyone under attack could have made their way through without once being exposed to bowshot from the cliffs surrounding them. It was much more to Quill's liking, but still, there was something in the air that made him tense and nervous, a feeling of hushed expectancy.

"I don't want to sound alarmist, but make sure your weapons are easy at hand," he said. He reached over his shoulder and pulled out a long length of wood. He always liked to carry a non-lethal option, so he had liberated the handle of one of the axes that they'd taken from the woodcutters. It was solid ash and almost as thick as his wrist, and could be just as lethal as a sword if you knew what you were doing—but it gave him the ability to simply incapacitate if he so chose.

"One step ahead of you, buddy," Rocket said. He still had the cudgel he'd used in the forest, and looked far too eager to start cracking heads.

Slowly, they made their way through the stone forest. The boulders were tall enough that even Groot couldn't see over them, so they were forced to scout around each one. Quill froze as he caught a flicker of movement out of the corner of his eye, a black shadow that flitted from one stone to another. Something tugged at his trousers, and he looked down to find Rocket trying to get his attention.

"I know, I saw it," Quill whispered. "Don't let on that we've spotted whatever it is. I'm keeping my eyes on it, and right now it's behind the third rock to the left."

"Ah, are we talking about the same thing?"

Quill followed Rocket's gaze to the right and saw another shadow, and then from behind there was a soft "I am Groot."

"I think we might be surrounded," Rocket said.

Suddenly there was movement all around them. The largest of the shadowy figures was almost as big as Quill, but they ranged to no larger than Rocket, and all of them flitted from stone to stone with the same fluid grace. Given the figures' constant movement, it was hard to get a count, but there were at least a dozen—maybe two.

"Let's try and get to the other end and maybe find some higher ground," Rocket hissed. "We can make them come at us that way."

Quill nodded, always happy to bow to the raccoonoid's tactical genius. They hurried though the pass, trying to look in every direction at once, so absorbed with their pursuers that it took Quill a moment to notice that the pass ended in a soaring cliff. He stopped cold, eyes following the almost vertical wall, staring in wonder at the intricate scaffolding that clung to the rock and supported a dozen huts that hung from the ropes like grapes on a vine. The only way up was a rope ladder that he imagined could be rolled up in case of attack, and at its foot stood three women in red monks' robes. The one in the middle stepped forward and spoke in a strong, clear voice.

"Strangers, you are trespassing in the Valley of the Lotus. We do not seek violence, and if you turn back now from whence you came, you will not be harmed."

The speaker was an older woman, perhaps in her sixties, with long, flowing white hair that contrasted sharply with the shaved heads of her two younger companions.

Quill gave her his most charming smile and raised his hands peacefully.

"Look, we mean no harm. We're looking for a friend. She . . ."

"You have no friends here, beast." One of the younger women spoke, fire burning in her wide eyes, her shoulders quivering with suppressed rage. "Leave now, or be whipped the way curs deserve."

"Hang on a minute," Quill said, angry despite himself. "I don't know what your problem is, but I don't really appreciate your tone."

"Last warning, dog."

"Kasara!" the older woman snapped. "That will be enough."

"Thank you," Quill said.

The younger woman flushed.

"It is not enough," she argued. "They must leave. Now. This a security matter and the decision rests with me."

The older woman frowned, but nodded. "So be it."

Kasara pointed back the way that the Quill and his companions had come.

"Last warning. Go now or suffer the consequences."

"And suppose we don't?" Rocket asked, his hackles raised.

Quill knew the raccoonoid hated animal names being used as insults, and that his temper would be on a hair trigger right now. "What are you going to do about it?"

Kasara's smile was cold enough to be glacial.

"I hoped that you'd say that."

She reached into her robe and Quill prepared to dive behind the stone to his right if she drew any sort of projectile weapon. Instead she pulled out an ornate golden horn.

"Last chance. Are you sure you won't leave?"

Quill shook his head. "All we want is some answers."

"So be it."

She raised the horn to her lips and blew. A long mellow note echoed from the cliffs, and then everything happened at once.

There was a blur of motion to Quill's left, and he only just managed to bring his weapon up in time to block a vicious blow from a rice flail wielded with dangerous precision. He flicked the end of the shaft back up, catching his attacker in the pit of the stomach. He cracked his stick over its head as it doubled up in pain and slumped to the ground, letting Quill see it for the first time. *It* was bundled in a shapeless black robe, a deep hood covering its face. He reached down to see what was underneath the cowl, but before he could, there was a shout from up ahead.

"Quill, come on!"

Quill straightened up and hurried to his companions.

They were completely surrounded now, and the shadowy figures were becoming more daring. Two leaped on Groot, bringing lengths of wood bashing down with furious blows. Groot roared and grabbed one in either hand, tearing them away from his body and hurling them back into the shadows. Rocket was beset on all sides, his cudgel darting into the path of blow after blow, teeth bared in a feral snarl. Before Quill could reach Rocket, he found himself fighting for his own life against multiple attackers. Twirling the ash handle, he lunged and parried, knocking aside kicks, punches, and clubs, and sending his foes sprawling with brutal blows.

A small round object came sailing out from behind one of the stones and smashed at his feet, sending a cloud of acrid, noxious smoke billowing towards his face. Quill began to cough, tears running from his eyes as he struggled to breathe. More of the smoke bombs rained down, and the fumes surrounded them, making it hard to see and harder to breath. Groot seemed oblivious, but Rocket was closer to the ground and his acute sense of smell became a weakness as each breath exposed him to more of whatever it was in the air. Still choking, Quill ripped a swatch of fabric from the cloak of one of the unconscious enemies and covered his mouth and nose, bringing some relief. Rocket saw what he was doing and followed suit, the makeshift masks giving them enough protection to continue to defend themselves while the smoke began to clear.

Whoever their attackers were, they were skilled enough, showing mastery of whatever weapons they bore, and they were fast. But they couldn't match the experience and strength of the three travelers and, one by one, they fell before them. There must have been twenty unconscious bodies scattered around them when a larger figure leaped out at Quill. This one was clad in a white robe, and made the others look like they'd been moving in slow motion. It was all Quill could do to defend himself against the whirlwind of fists and feet that he found himself swept up in. One punch snapped his axe handle cleanly in half, and just missed dong the same to his jaw. Quill's awkward evasion saved him as a kick he hadn't even seen coming lashed past his face and connected with the rock behind him, cracking off chunks of stone.

Lowering his shoulder, Quill bulldozed into the robed figure, sending it staggering backwards. His breath was coming in short, sharp gasps, hindered by his mask, and he took advantage of the brief respite to tear it from his face. He braced himself for the next attack, but his foe wasn't moving.

"Quill?"

The voice was as familiar to him as his own, and he felt memories flooding back.

"Gamora?"

The figure took a step towards him, before reaching up and pulling back the hood of her robe. Her eyes met his, wide with both surprise and—he saw with a sinking feeling in his stomach—anger.

"What do you think you're doing?" she asked. "You shouldn't be here! And what have you done to my pupils?"

"Your *pupils*?" Quill asked stupidly.

Instead of replying, she simply knelt next to one of the prone figures and gently pulled the cowl of its robe back. Quill gasped in shock, his face flushing at the sight of a young girl, barely in her teens, her eye blackened and swelling from one of his blows.

"I was fighting little gi—" he cut off, seeing the anger build on Gamora's face. "I mean, I was fighting children? I didn't know!"

"There is a lot you don't know, Quill." She sighed. "I guess you should come with me so I can remedy that."

Without another word she turned and stalked towards the suspended village, not even waiting to see if the three companions were following.

CHAPTER 8

The huts were surprisingly spacious inside. It probably helped that they had left Groot down on the ground, but still, there were five of them sitting comfortably around a low table. It was a shame that the atmosphere was as cold as ice—in a strictly emotional sense—the chill was emanating from the young woman sitting directly across from Rocket and Quill.

"Let us be clear," Kasara said. "If it were up to me, you'd be walking—or crawling—out of the valley by now."

Rocket half-laughed, half-snarled at her.

"Seems like you gave it your best shot, and yet here we are."

"Don't get too cocky, rodent," Kasara said. "We'd only just gotten started."

"Kasara!" The older woman had been sitting quietly, but when she spoke her voice had the weight of absolute authority. "You will be civil to our guests."

"Abbess . . ."

"Do you understand me?"

Kasara hung her head, but Quill could still make out the splotches of red on her cheeks.

"Yes, Abbess. Forgive me."

Rocket grinned at Kasara, but his smile faded as the Abbess turned the full force of her gaze on him.

"Rocket, you would do well to work on your manners, too," she said. "Kasara is right. We do have other ways of dealing with intruders, and you are only here as a favor to Sister Gamora."

For once, Rocket didn't have a quick reply at hand, and Quill's estimation of the Abbess went up a notch. He couldn't remember the last time the raccoonoid had been quelled with a look.

"May I be excused?" Kasara asked. "I have duties to attend to."

"If you must," the Abbess said, sighing.

Once Kasara was gone, the Abbess turned back to Quill and Rocket.

"Forgive her. Her life has not been easy, and she has good reason to be distrustful of strangers," said the Abbess. "But she has a good heart, and she would do anything to protect this monastery and the girls here."

"Tell us about this place," Quill said. "I've heard wild tales, but I'd rather get the real story."

The Abbess smiled. "That shows wisdom. There has been a monastery on this site for almost a thousand years. We were founded with one purpose—to provide a safe haven for young girls who had been orphaned or who had been victims of brutality. We teach them the skills they will need to not only survive, but thrive, and then they leave us. Some girls decide to stay, like Kasara, and give back."

"Only girls?" Rocket asked. "Seems a bit unfair."

Both Gamora and the Abbess glared at him. Quill was

more than happy to see someone else at the receiving end of those looks; he wouldn't have wanted to be Rocket right now.

"Let me assure you that males have plenty of opportunities for advancement in our world, and one monastery dedicated to women is not going to disadvantage men in any way," the Abbess said.

"So, how does Gamora fit in here, then?" Quill asked.

"When Sister Gamora arrived, she wanted no more than a place of quiet meditation where she could ignore the outside world. Once she became aware of our mission, however, she volunteered to help train our acolytes, and to rescue those who could benefit from our help," she said. "There are some who aren't as enthusiastic as we are about seeing young women rescued. Gamora is very good at . . . persuading them."

"I bet she is," Quill said.

"I know as well as anyone how cruel this universe can be to women, and what it feels like to be powerless," Gamora said softly. "I saw a chance to make sure that these girls, at least, would escape that fate. But the question is, why are you here, Quill?"

Quill couldn't meet her eyes. "I can see why that would be something that makes you feel fulfilled. Now I feel bad for what I'm about to ask," he said, as he went on to explain the nomad threat and what the Duke had asked of him.

"Do you know what you are asking of me?" she asked when he had finished. "I have found a place where the skills I was taught for the sake of destruction can be used to bring peace and healing. I don't know whether I can throw that away."

"Sister Gamora, why don't you take our visitors on a tour of the monastery?" the Abbess asked. "That way, they might get a better understanding of what it is we are doing, and why it is so important to you. I think it will be good for you, too. A reminder."

Gamora looked like she wanted to argue, but all she said was, "Yes, mother."

Rocket and Quill followed Gamora to the door. The basket that had brought them up from the ground was still waiting, and Gamora unhinged the wooden gate so they could board it. She grabbed a dangling rope and began to pull it down hand over hand. The basket was suspended from an elaborate system of pulley and gears. It looked to Quill as if even a child would have been able to pull up the basket and their own weight—and Gamora was no child.

As they clambered up onto the plateau above the cliff face, Quill saw that it stretched back hundreds of feet and featured a dozen long, low buildings made of stone. The buildings were arranged around the edges to make way for a wide open space in which scores of children were running through a series of exercises. While they were moving at a deliberate pace, Quill could recognize techniques from some of the most vicious martial arts he'd ever come across. Their execution was flawless, and Quill had no doubt that when they returned to normal speed they would be formidable foes indeed. He wasn't surprised to see Kasara leading them, either. She had the air of a drill sergeant. Gamora walked over to her and bowed, Kasara returning the courtesy. Quill noted that Kasara bowed just as deeply, which he assumed meant she saw the other woman as an equal.

"Sister, the Abbess has asked me to show these men what we do here," Gamora said. "Would you be so kind as to help me give them a demonstration?"

"I am expected to waste my time on them?" Kasara asked incredulously. Gamora let her vent, and Kasara gradually ran out of steam. "Well, if the Abbess commands it, who am I to argue?"

Kasara issued a series of commands and the children rapidly moved into a circle with the two women inside, about twenty feet from the nearest child. Gamora beckoned Quill and Rocket over, and they joined the circle.

"Touch?" Kasara asked.

"I think so. I don't want to scare these poor fragile men," Gamora said, a teasing note in her voice.

"Agreed. On my mark. Mark!"

What followed was half dance, half brawl, as beautiful as it was terrifying. Kasara whirled into a perfectly executed spinning back kick, only for Gamora to block her foot inches from her face. She dropped into a leg sweep, knocking Kasara from her feet, but somehow the other woman turned the tumble into a flip that saw her land back on her feet and in position to attack. As she threw a punch, Gamora grabbed her hand and pivoted, twisting Kasara's arm up behind her back. With a lithe twist, Kasara reversed the hold, and now it was Gamora straining against a brutal arm bar. The advantage seesawed back and forth between the two women, Kasara throwing Gamora over her shoulder, only for Gamora to come bounding back up and drive her opponent back with a series of crescent kicks. There was one last flurry of blows, and then Kasara was on her knees with the tips of Gamora's rigid fingers digging into the hollow of her throat.

"I nearly had you that time," Kasara said.

"Nearly doesn't count, sister, not in combat." Gamora reached down and pulled Kasara to her feet and they embraced. "Well fought, I am proud of you."

Kasara laughed. "You should be—you taught me most of the things I tried."

"That was incredible," Quill said as he joined them.

Gamora smiled at his words, but Kasara gave him a cold glare.

"I don't really care what you think," she snapped.

Quill flushed, angry despite himself.

"You're pretty good in an exhibition, but I wonder why you sent your students against us to do your job for you," he sneered. "Not so good when it comes to the real thing?"

Kasara took a step towards him, fists clenched at her side. Gamora reached out and grabbed the other woman's arm.

"Don't be a fool, Quill. Kasara would have loved nothing more than to deal with you herself. Surely you can see that?" Quill had to admit she had a point. "It's a part of the students' training to experience real combat. But we don't let them be part of it until we are certain they are ready."

"That's pretty brutal," Quill said.

"It's a brutal world. And some of them don't survive. But, would it be better if we sent them back out into it with a false idea of what they were capable of?"

"I still think it's a bad idea. They're only children."

"Let me show you their full capabilities. Then we will see if you think of them as 'only' anything."

"What do you mean?" Quill asked warily.

Gamora's only reply was to clap her hands and say one word. "Ansari!"

One of the students trotted over. She was short and slight, her head coming up only to Quill's chest. Her reddish brown hair was cut short and framed fine-boned, fox-like features.

"This man doesn't think you can fight. Would you like to show him otherwise?"

"Yes, mistress!" Ansari exclaimed.

"Hang on," Quill said, not liking where this was going. "I am not fighting a child."

"Scared of a little girl, Quill?" Rocket jeered.

"It's okay, Quill, you can go easy if you want. I don't think you'll need to, but that's up to you," Gamora said. "We want you to see how talented these 'children' are. Ansari is my personal apprentice, and I think she will give you some much needed exercise. Unless Rocket is right . . ."

"Fine," Quill snapped. "Let's do this."

The words were barely out of his mouth when Ansari drove her fist into his stomach. As he doubled up, she punched him in the nose, bringing tears of pain. She threw another punch but he caught this one and squeezed, bending her fist back and forcing her to her knees.

"Seriously? That's what you teach them here? To sucker punch people?" he gasped.

"I teach them to win," Gamora said. "That's what matters. They will usually be facing someone bigger and stronger, so they need to seize on every advantage that they can possibly find."

"That's right," Rocket said. "And the bigger they are, the harder they fall. You get him, kid! Strike a blow for those of us that come in small packages."

As quick as a snake, Ansari flung her body around, driving both feet into Quill's knees and breaking his hold. He brought his foot down to stamp on her, but she rolled away and was on her feet before he could blink. She came at him again and again, throwing kicks and punches with reckless abandon, her anger overwhelming her training. He was handicapped by the fact that he didn't want to hurt her, and she not only knew it, but was using it against him. She was able to concentrate on offense, often leaving herself open in order to strike at him.

He saw a dozen opportunities to take her down, but each time he held back, and he paid for it as she hit him again and again.

"Come on, Quill, what are you doing?" Rocket yelled. "Finish her."

"Shut up, Rocket!" Quill grunted. "It's okay for *you* to say that, you'd be picking on someone your own size."

Quill wasn't sure who was more offended by that comment, the raccoonoid or Ansari. She let out a cry of rage and redoubled her attack. Quill blocked most of her blows, but more than one got through, striking him in tender places that left him wincing, tears of a pain in his eyes.

"Okay, that's it," he snarled.

As she came at him again he stepped inside her blow, ignoring the punch that he took in the ribs. There was a look of panic in her eyes as he closed in on her and brought his superior strength into play. His fingers dug into her arms as he spun her and wrapped his arm around her neck. Flexing his muscles, he squeezed, bringing pressure to bear on the arteries in her throat, while being careful not to crush her larynx. As the flow of blood to her brain began to slacken, she struggled against his grip.

"Yield," Quill said.

Her only response was to throw her head back to try and headbutt him in the chin, but he was too strong for her. She tried everything—stamping on his instep, driving her elbow back—but Quill was in too good a position, and had complete control.

"Yield," he demanded again, squeezing even harder.

"Never," she choked out.

"You really *are* Gamora's apprentice," he said admiringly. "So be it."

Slowly Ansari's struggles began to weaken, then slowly and finally she blacked out, going limp in his arms. Gently, Quill laid her down on the grass, and checked her airways. It was a measure of the fight she had put up that he did so very carefully, keeping out of her reach as much as was possible—in case she was bluffing.

"Well, I won't say that was fun," he said. "Talk about a chip off the old block. You've done a great job training her."

Kasara was looking at him appraisingly, as if seeing him properly for the first time.

"Maybe you aren't as bad as I thought," she said. "A lot of men would have lost their tempers and lashed out. But, you . . . you were careful not to inflict any unnecessary pain."

"It's one thing to fight; it's another to enjoy hurting people," Quill said uncomfortably, surprised at her praise. "She fought well, and I just tried to protect myself without hurting her too much. In a few years, I won't have that luxury—she'll be too good for anyone fighting her to hold back."

Kasara didn't say anything else, but for the rest of the day he would catch her eyes upon him, and wonder what exactly she was thinking.

CHAPTER 9

"**A**s you can see, there is more to this place than just learning to fight," Gamora said.

They were watching a group of young girls learning the intricate symbols of a form of mathematics that bore a striking resemblance to algebra. As they looked on, one of the sisters was writing on a large chalkboard and the students were industriously scribbling away. Quill shook his head; some of that math was beyond him—not that he'd ever been a big fan of the subject.

"When they leave here, they will be capable of doing whatever they want to," Gamora continued. "We will even set them up with enough funds to start a small business. Most of them end up not only paying us back, but making an additional donation to help support the next generation of students."

"When I saw those huts hanging off the cliff face, I wouldn't have imagined all this was here," Quill said. "Which, I imagine, is the point."

"Exactly," Gamora said. "We keep all this hidden from those who would take it away from us. And, the way that the huts are placed acts as an excellent last line of defense."

Quill imagined trying to climb up to the huts with warriors like Gamora and Kasara, or even Ansari, waiting above, ready to hurl down death. He shuddered at the thought.

"I can see how they would be," he said. "I'm impressed by what the sisters have achieved here, and I can understand why you feel at home."

"And you understand why I can't just leave?" she asked. "It's not that I don't want to help you, but I just can't."

Quill reached out and took her hand. For a moment she tensed as if she were going to pull away, and then she relaxed.

"I do understand, Gamora, and I'm not going to hold it against you. What you have here is worth defending."

"I think you should go, daughter." The Abbess had been so quiet that Quill had almost forgotten she was there, and when she spoke, it startled him enough to make him jump slightly.

"You think I should go, mother?" Gamora asked. "Why?"

"Because you will be doing the same work as you do here," she replied.

"I don't understand."

"How many orphans will the nomad invasion leave behind? How many terrified young girls will there be with no one to turn to? How many are there already?" the Abbess asked. "You need to be where you can make the most differ-ence. We both know that your talents are bigger than this, no matter how important what we do here is. I have others who can do your work here, like Kasara, but you are the most likely to change things out there."

"But . . ."

"But nothing, daughter," the Abbess said, iron in her voice. "If you can help turn back this invasion, you will save countless lives. And you will find plenty of children to send to us for help—children who would otherwise have no hope."

"But mother, . . . I don't want to abandon you," Gamora said. "You've done so much for me."

"You won't be abandoning us, daughter, you'll be fulfilling our mission," the Abbess said, smiling. "And you know that you will always be welcome here."

Gamora argued for a little bit longer, but the Abbess was implacable, and Quill knew that it was already decided. The rest was just talking.

When they got down to the bottom of the cliff, Groot was surrounded by children. They were climbing all over him, tugging at his leaves and swinging from his branches. The sound of their laughter echoed around the valley, and was matched by the broad smile on Groot's face.

"Sorry, big guy, it's time to get going," Rocket said. "Cleanse yourself of these parasites and let's make a move."

"I am Groot."

"Yeah, okay, so they aren't the most repulsive rug rats I've ever seen," Rocket grumbled. "But, still, time to go."

With incredible gentleness, Groot began to pull the children off and place them on the ground. A few complained, but most seemed incredibly calm, as if Groot's mere presence was a mood-altering substance. He walked over to his companions and reached out, brushing Gamora's cheek with a tendril.

"I am Groot."

Gamora smiled at him. "I'm happy to see you again, too."

"Isn't this sweet?" Rocket said, but there was no venom in his voice—only affection. "We're getting the band back together!"

"Now we just need to find Drax," Quill said. "I honestly have no idea where he might be."

"Actually, about that . . ." Gamora said. "I don't know where to find him, but I know what direction he was headed in. We ended up traveling together for a little while after we left you at the ship."

Quill felt an irrational sting of jealousy, but tried to sound calm. "I didn't know that," he said. "But that helps. As long as he didn't decide to change course."

"Not likely. You know Drax, it takes a lot to get him to deviate from a straight line," she said, and Quill nodded. "He would have kept marching until he found a place to call home, and the gods help anyone who got in his way."

"And which way was that?" Quill asked.

"That's the bad news," Gamora said. "When I last saw him, he was headed into the wilderness, which is all sand and nothing until you reach the Broken Hills—and they are over a month's hard marching from here. There wouldn't have been anything to capture his interest before he reached them."

"I don't have weeks," Quill said. "I'm running out of time."

"I do have an idea," Gamora said. "It's a long shot, though."

"I'm not sure what choice we have at this point," Quill said. "A long shot is better than no shot."

"At the monastery we have tired to preserve books and histories that would have otherwise been lost or forgotten," Gamora said. "Our monastery has been here a long time, and there are a number of books in our library that mention a now-extinct race that tamed some sort of winged creature and used it for transport. I don't know whether it is a myth, or garbled accounts of gliders or something similar, or whether they actually did ride giant birds. But there are enough mentions of it for me to think there's something to it."

"You're right," Rocket said. "That's a very long shot."

"I said it was," Gamora retorted. "If you have any better ideas, feel free to share."

"And where did these aviators live?" Quill asked. "I certainly hope nearby."

Gamora smiled. "Exactly. This very mountain. Right at the top."

Quill tilted his head back to stare at the slopes above them. The peak was so far away that all he could see were clouds.

"That's just wonderful. Because I love heights so much." He squared his shoulders and picked up his pack. "No time like the present, I suppose."

* * *

They climbed for hours. At the beginning, there were well-defined paths to follow, some with ropes strung through iron bolts that had been drilled into the stone. As they moved farther up the slopes, though, the signs of human presence began to fade and the well-trodden paths became nothing more than winding goat tracks. The air began to thin and the travelers struggled more and more to breathe—with the exception of Groot, who seemed oblivious to the changing altitude. By the time the sun began to set, they were exhausted, and there was no arguing when Quill suggested making camp for the night. They managed to find a flat piece of ground surrounded by scraggly bushes that provided a bit of cover from the cold wind whistling around them. After gathering up enough brush to build a small fire, the companions huddled around it.

"Isn't this fun," Rocket said. "I've missed this. Haven't you?"

"I am Groot."

"I knew you'd feel that way, big guy," Rocket said.

"Actually, I really *have* missed this," Quill said. "The Duke's court was a lot of fun, but no one there had quite your way with words."

The others laughed.

"Seriously, though, it is nice to see you all again," Quill said.

"You aren't going to get all emotional on us are you, Quill?" Rocket asked. He made a retching noise.

"I hope Drax will be as happy to see us," Gamora said. "You never know how he's going to react."

"Yeah, he might be so angry to see us that he crushes us," Rocket paused for effect, "or so happy to see us he hugs us . . . and crushes us."

"Very true," Gamora said, chuckling. "But I've missed him. I've missed all of you."

"Fine," Rocket grumbled, "I might have missed you . . . a little."

"I am a Groot."

As they kept talking, Gamora leaned forward and scratched something in the dirt. Quill could barely make it out.

Don't say anything, but there is someone hiding in the bushes.

Quill's eyes widened, but he managed not to react beyond that. Keeping one ear on the conversation, he listened carefully with the other. *There.* The one with the oddly-shaped leaves. Slowly he began to inch his way around the fire, moving ever closer. When he was within reach, he made a show of standing up slowly and stretching.

"I'm going to fetch some more wood. I won't be long."

He casually turned, and then lunged for the bush, reaching in with both hands and closing them around a spitting, squirming creature. He pulled it free, holding it at arm's length to avoid its vicious attempts to swipe at him. Just then the fire flared up, and Quill almost dropped his captive as he recognized her.

"Ansari!" he exclaimed.

"What?" Gamora leaped to her feet. "What are you doing here?"

Ansari didn't answer, and stared sullenly back at Quill.

"If I put you down, will you behave?" He shook her slightly. "Will you?"

She nodded, and he placed her on the ground. For a moment he thought she was going to bolt, but before she could Gamora grabbed her arm.

"What are you doing here? You need to explain yourself."

"I'm your apprentice! I am meant to be with you, watching your back," Ansari said.

"This is far too dangerous a journey for you. I left you behind because I didn't want you getting hurt."

"It's not fair, mistress. You told me that my training was to prepare me for the real world, and that I needed to find out what real combat was—but then when you come out here, you leave me behind." She sounded close to tears. "Don't you think I'm good enough? I thought you were proud of me."

Gamora seemed genuinely taken aback.

"It's not that, Ansari. You are the best student I have ever had," she said gently. "It's just that you are too young for this."

"And how young were you when you first fought for your life, mistress?"

"That's not the point, Ansari," Gamora snapped.

"Isn't it? You've been telling me since you started teaching me that you wanted me to be able to make my own decisions, control my own life. Well, this is what I want. I want to help you stop anyone else losing their parents . . . like I did."

"I think she's got you there, Gamora," Rocket said.

Gamora glared at him, and then her shoulders slumped.

"Fine, I suppose she does." She turned to her student. "But you need to obey every command you are given, even if you don't agree. We've been doing this sort of thing for a long time. Agreed?"

The girl's face lit up. "Oh, yes! You won't regret this, I promise."

"If you keep me awake any longer you'll be the one regretting things," Rocket growled, showing his teeth.

Ansari looked at him with wide eyes, then scuttled over to the other side of the fire and curled up near Gamora's bedroll. Rocket winked at Quill and settled down next to Groot, and was soon snoring softly.

The ground was rocky and uncomfortable, and it took Quill a long time to get to sleep. When he finally awoke, he was stiff and sore, and his eyes felt like they were full of sand. The group didn't even have coffee to help them wake him up. After a perfunctory wash, they set off again, Ansari indecently enthusiastic for that time of the morning. She seemed to have twice as much energy as the rest of them, and had to be called back a number of times when she got too far ahead. But Quill had to admit that her high spirits were infectious, and gradually she even got Rocket smiling and cracking jokes with her. They were halfway up a particularly nasty slope when Ansari, still laughing at the punch line of Rocket's latest joke, suddenly stopped and frowned.

"What's that noise?" she asked.

"What noise?" Rocket asked. Then his eyes narrowed. "Oh, hell."

The rumbling grew louder, coming from upslope but getting rapidly closer.

"Brace yourselves!" Quill yelled.

Below him he heard a muffled, "I am Groot!" and then the snow and rocks hit them, sweeping them down the slope. They had rounded a corner only a few hundred feet below, and Quill knew that a straight line down the slope they were on would end in a sickening drop. He reached desperately for a ragged looking shrub, his hands closing convulsively around its trunk, rough bark abrading his skin, and for a moment thought he was safe. Then, there was a ripping noise that he felt through his hands more than he heard it; the bush pulled free of the flinty soil, and he was again sliding towards death. Suddenly, he came to an abrupt halt hard enough to knock the breath from him. The snow and rocks were still pounding him, pushing him up against the barrier, but it didn't yield, and cradled him until the worst was over.

Once he had caught his breath, he opened his eyes, wincing at the bright sunlight. He was suspended in a web of branches, and mere inches from his were a big pair of eyes and a happy smile.

"I am Groot."

Groot had literally put down roots deep in the side of the mountain, while others had wound around a nearby boulder. He had grown a number of extra arms—or perhaps they were branches, Quill was never sure—and had spread them like wings, blocking off the slope. Gamora and Ansari clung together close to his trunk, while Rocket hung upside down at the left-hand edge of Groot's reach, a tendril wrapped around his ankles and holding him safe.

"Let me down," Rocket yelled. "Right now."

The tendril suddenly unclenched, and Rocket dropped to the ground, only just missing landing on his head.

"Yeah, thanks for that," he grumbled. "But I guess I owe you one, big guy."

"I think we all do," Gamora said. She and Ansari descended much more gracefully than the raccoonoid. "It is a long way down."

Quill clapped Groot on the shoulder, wincing slightly at the splinters.

"Good work, you saved us all."

"I am Groot," he said, beaming.

"You sure are," Quill said, "and I, for one, am very glad of it."

CHAPTER 10

Quill dragged himself up the last few feet of cliff face, and then over the edge. Rolling onto his back, he simply laid there for a few minutes, trying to catch his breath. Every muscle ached, and he was covered with bruises and abrasions. Finally, he staggered to his feet and joined the others, who stood waiting for him over near a cluster of low, stone huts.

"Glad you could join us," Rocket said. "You humans and your lack of claws. It's sad, really."

"Didn't stop us," Gamora said, motioning to her student. "We beat all of you."

Ansari smiled at her. "We had an advantage—we aren't weighed down by our egos."

"I think I liked you better when you were too scared to speak," Quill said, but he was grinning, too. "So, what's all this?"

"There used to be a tribe living up here. The details are fuzzy, but from what I have heard, they died from some plague." She saw Quill flinch. "Don't worry, it was decades ago."

"And they tamed the creatures you were talking about?" Rocket asked. "If they even existed, of course."

"That's right. They had some secret method that they refused to share, but if we can find it anywhere, it will be here," Gamora said. "Now let's split up and search the huts to see if we can find anything that looks useful."

Quill looked at the squat buildings, and then at Groot.

"Groot, perhaps you should wait out here and guard our belongings?"

"I am Groot."

Groot went and stood near their pile of gear, then turned his face up to the sunshine. The rest of them made their way over to the huts, taking one each. Quill chose the largest one that sat in the middle of the rest, like a planet surrounded by its moons. Ornately carved doors nestled in a low-linteled opening that gave way to cool darkness as Quill stepped inside. The hut was built on a hexagonal pattern, giving it a vaguely insectile feel. The building gave no sense of being someone's home, instead having an official air. Moldering maps were pinned to the walls of one of the rooms, and in another a rack of swords still gleamed, as if they'd just come from the forge. But the biggest shock was the shattered remains of what were unmistakably primitive calculating machines. A jumble of transistors and fragments of glass lay on the floor near a table surrounded by ominous but faded stains. Quill tried to piece together what had happened. There was no real damage to anything other than the computer, so whatever had done it had come with a very specific mission—this was no random act of violence.

Quill knew that he was merely speculating, but the side-by-side existence of a computer with a far more primitive material like parchment pointed to a society just starting to open up new possibilities, not a well-established one, and the swords showed that they hadn't been as invested in weapons development—meaning they probably hadn't been militaristic or expansionary. So who would have wanted to do this? A rival culture worried about these technological advances, and wanting to nip them in the bud? That would indicate a level of forward planning that was downright concerning on a planet like this. Quill shook his head. He might never find out what had happened, and he was on a deadline—he had no time for mysteries. If he survived the next few months, there would be plenty of time to come back. Resolved, he continued searching.

It was in the second-to-last room that he found what he was looking for. The whole room was taken up with a massive rack of pegs, and from each hung a harness that—while different in size and shape still suggested a horse's bridle—and a flutelike instrument. Despite its obvious age, the leather of the harnesses was still soft and flexible, and the brass fittings were untarnished. Quill brought five of the harnesses and five of the instruments back out into the sunshine and joined Groot, laying the harnesses out on the grass while he waited for the others to return.

"Well, we have the harnesses, what about the steeds?"

Rocket asked when he got back. "Any ideas where we might find them?"

Shyly, Ansari pulled out a rolled out parchment.

"I think I do," she said. "I found this in one of the huts."

"Great work!" Quill said.

Ansari blushed. "I'm not sure you are going to like what it says. As far as I can work out, they're up there."

Quill followed the line of her finger and groaned in dismay. She was pointing at the very highest peak of the mountain, three or four hundred feet above them, and high enough to be wreathed in cloud.

"More climbing. Well, the sooner we start, the sooner we'll get there," he said.

In the end, it took them the best part of the day to reach the top of the mountain. The only things that made the climb possible were the handholds and occasional steps hacked into the mountainside. The companions were obviously not the first people to come that way, and at one time it was likely a well-traveled pathway. The climb ended at a rock shelf that stuck out from the mountainside about fifty feet below the pinnacle. There was another abandoned hut and a large doorway in the mountainside. Quill couldn't tell if it was artificial in its entirety, but if it had started as the mouth of a natural cave, it had been widened and adorned with carved friezes showing insectile bipeds engaged in activities ranging from hunting to feasting.

The travelers cautiously entered the doorway and stopped in amazement. The inside of the peak was completely hollowed out, falling away from the ledge on which they stood to unfathomable depths, and reaching up to a tiny square of daylight far above. The walls moved and rippled, and for a moment Quill thought that they had triggered some ancient trap that would bring the cavern collapsing on top of them. Then his eyes adjusted, and he saw the movement for what it was.

"It seems we have found our steeds," Gamora said, her voice breathless with wonder.

The walls were crawling with thousands of winged creatures, each with a body as big as a knight's charger and with a wingspan to match. They looked like a cross between bat and bee—long, membraned wings covered with iridescent scales, and bodies covered with a delicate fuzz. Their heads had an almost comical appearance with curled, fernlike antennas, but there was nothing funny about the jagged fangs that were revealed when they opened their mouths to yawn, or let out low mournful cries—or to snap at any neighbor that dared come too close.

"I'm not sure I really want to ride one of them," Rocket said. "They don't look all that friendly. How do you plan on getting close enough to get a harness on one without getting your hand—or your head—taken off?"

Quill had to admit that the raccoonoid had a point. He'd

had enough trouble with his horse, and he wasn't really that keen on getting near any of these creatures. It was Ansari who gave them the answer. She pulled out one of the flutes and gave it an experimental blow. The sound that emerged sounded much like the cries of the winged beasts around them, and encouraged, she started to play a simple tune. There was a stirring among the creatures closest to them, and one emerged from the swarm and crawled down to the ledge. Reflexively Quill reached for his sword, but Gamora clamped her hand down on his before he could draw it, her fingers like bands of steel.

"Wait," she whispered.

Ansari took one of the harnesses and slowly approached the creature, one careful step at a time. It watched her approach through six emerald compound eyes, and as she reached it, it lowered its head to allow her to slide the harness over it. It was a matter of adjusting two straps before it fit perfectly, and then Ansari turned and gave them a broad, triumphant smile.

"Great apprentice you have there," Quill said quietly. "You should be very proud."

"I am," Gamora said. She played a tune on her own flute, and soon had another of the creatures in harness. Each of the travelers followed suit, Quill watching in a sort of horrified wonder as Groot partly absorbed the flute into the cluster of branches at the crown of his head and then played it without having it anywhere near his mouth.

"So, what now?" Gamora asked.

They had mounted the creatures—the narrow waists behind the wings a perfect place to sit—and had been able to get the creatures to move around using the reins. But Quill didn't know what other commands the creatures might be expecting.

"Well, I guess there's only one thing to try now," he muttered. "Faint heart never won fair lady."

He directed his beast to the edge of the ledge, trying not to stare down into the chasm in case his nerves failed. With a sudden shout he dug his heels into the creature's sides and leaned forward as it lurched out over the brink. For a moment he thought he had killed them both as they hurtled straight down, wind whistling through his hair, but then there was a whip-crack of sound and a jaw-clicking jolt as the creature extended its wings to their full span and they filled with air. Their descent slowed and then the huge wings began to beat. The beast didn't so much seem to fly back up towards the ledge as claw its way back up through the air. There was a definite updraft coming from the depths of the cavern, and as the beast came level with the ledge, it almost hovered, using only the occasional lazy beat of its wings to stay stationary.

"What a rush!" Quill yelled to the others over the vast flapping sound. "That was amazing. Come on, you should all give it a go."

One by one, the other travelers urged their mounts over

the edge. Each one experienced the same sickening drop and the same laborious ascent. Groot must have weighed a good two or three times as much as Quill, and his fall seemed to go on forever—for a moment Quill feared they might have lost him—but soon they were all in the air and circling one another. Through trial and error they worked out how to direct their steeds through the air, and Quill gave his mount another heel in the side and sent it towards the square of sunlight far above. As they approached, the opening seemed to grow larger and larger, proving wide enough to fit three of the beasts flying wingtip to wingtip. Quill grinned as they emerged, blinking in the bright daylight, and he gave his mount the freedom to fly. It opened its mouth and let out another bugling cry, this one filled with unbridled joy. Their mounts answering their leader's summons, the others followed, and soon they all wheeled and circled the top of the mountain, discovering just what their steeds were capable of. The creatures were surprisingly agile for their size, capable of turning almost on a dime. They wouldn't obey any commands that asked too much of them, but what they would do was amazing. Each of the beasts showed itself able to pull out of dives so steep that they almost ended up brushing the ground, and was capable of astonishing bursts of speed. After an hour of sheer exuberance in which they gloried in the wonders of flight, and which was full of hard-fought races and mock dogfights, the creatures showed no signs of fatigue, and Quill realized that, with these wonderful creatures, he might just be able to keep his promise after all. Reluctantly, he flew alongside Gamora.

"I hate to say this, but we should get going soon," he yelled across at her.

"I know, but it's a shame," she yelled back. "Look at them, they are having so much fun."

She was right. Ansari and Groot were either racing or just keeping each other company, their mounts belly to belly with Groot hanging upside down. Rocket was putting his beast through its paces, working his way through a series of increasingly intricate turning patterns.

"So, where are we headed?" Quill asked Gamora. "You seemed to have some idea."

Gamora laughed. He'd missed that sound more than he wanted to admit. She pointed east; from their vantage point he could see that fertile fields gave way to flat plains, dry and dusty with only the occasional stunted tree breaking the monotony.

"If we fly in that direction long enough, we should reach the Broken Hills. It's not like we are going to miss them out there, with basically nothing else to see."

"Well, the sooner we start flying, the sooner we'll get there," Quill said.

"Is that how that works?" she asked, mocking him. "Okay, let's retrieve our gear and get going."

She brought two fingers up to her mouth and whistled, the piecing sound loud enough to get everyone's attention. With a series of hand gestures, she communicated the plan to the rest of the group, and almost as one, they wheeled around and followed her.

It soon became clear that Groot's beast was struggling with its burden, and it slowly fell behind, forcing the others to rein in their creatures and slow down.

"You're running out of time, aren't you," Rocket yelled to Quill.

"I am, but I don't know what to do about it."

"How about the big guy and I head back to the forest?"

"You're abandoning us?" Quill asked.

"Don't be silly," Rocket snapped. "We'll only hold you back, so let us do something useful. We'll see if we can find you some reinforcements in the forest, and then meet you in time for your rendezvous with the Duke."

"Reinforcements? From where?"

Rocket winked at him.

"Just trust me," he said. "The big guy is very good at making friends—and treaties go both ways."

"I hate it when you say that. It usually means I'm in big, big trouble," Quill complained. "Okay, you do that. Good luck."

Rocket lifted his hand in salute, then peeled off and rejoined Groot. The last thing Quill heard was a shout of "I am Groot" fading into the wind, and then they were gone.

The insect king looks down from his raised throne, staring at the captive standing before the dais. Through multi-faceted eyes that cut across multiple wavelengths of energy, the figure is a coruscating bloom of color. The king can see the huge heart beating, the fiery flow of blood through his veins, the power lurking in massive muscles as the captive stands absolutely still.

Despite being surrounded by insectoid warriors that loom over him, the captive shows no fear at all. Instead, it is the king's soldiers who seem nervous, shifting uneasily, as if unwilling to be in reach of those terrible arms. The captive has green skin, traced with scars and tattoos, the marks of a multitude of battles.

The king himself is no stranger to conflict—he has faced hundreds of challengers seeking to wrest away his throne according to the customs of his people. But for the first time, he wonders whether this will be the day that his reign ends. He reaches out with his mind, trying to learn more about this creature and reels back as waves of loss, grief, and rage crash into him.

The captive lifts his eyes and meets the king's gaze. There is a shared moment of understanding, and the king understands that the transfer of knowledge and emotion has not been one way, that the creature before him has learned just as much about the king as the king has about him. Worse, the captive *understands the challenge before him, the only way he will survive this encounter.*

The king stands, seven feet and more of rock-hard carapace, powerful muscle and razor sharp mandibles gleaming in the low light. Around the cavern, antennae quiver in anticipation, savoring the prospect of watching their ruler destroy this strange creature that has intruded into their world.

As he slowly descends from the dais, the king feels the string of an unfamiliar emotion. It is only when the captive smiles at him and beckons him closer that he recognizes it for what it is.

Fear.

CHAPTER 11

Now that Groot wasn't slowing them down, they ate up the miles with a steady pace. Quill watched carefully for any signs of fatigue among the animals, ready to give them a rest if needed. He knew that the time that they would save him was worth ensuring that they didn't founder. But on they flew, the only sign that they were flesh and blood rather than some incredibly efficient machine being the occasional drink. Even that didn't stop them completely, though, as they would simply dive at a body of water, pulling up at the last moment and skimming their open mouths along the surface. The first time it had happened Quill had nearly screamed, thinking his mount had developed a death wish and was going to drag him down with it into the watery depths. But once they knew what was going on, it was actually quite fun. Every so often a mouthful of water would come with a fish or two, and the lucky animal would devour them with relish, vicious teeth making short work of the meal. It was a reminder that these animals were not to be trifled with.

That didn't stop the riders from dozing off during the night, however, and the first time Quill came awake, he was disoriented and nearly fell from his mount. Pulling the map from his saddlebag he squinted at it in the starlight, and quickly looked around, taking in some of the landmarks he had noted earlier. He was happy to see that they were still on course.

"If you are going to do that, I'd suggest you clip yourself in," Gamora yelled to him, startling him so much he nearly fell all over again. He hadn't realized she had come so close.

She threw him a length of leather strap with a buckle at each end.

"You forgot to grab one of these."

Running the belt through the creature's harness left Quill feeling much more secure, and he settled back. When next he opened his eyes, the sun was rising and the ground below had changed. There were no more lakes and rivers, no green grass and thick foliage. They were well into the wasteland now, and Quill thanked whatever forces were looking out for him that he hadn't had to do this on foot. Of course, had he done so they would still be in the shadow of the mountains rather than approaching what had to be the Broken Hills. They were the only landmark visible, even from this height.

Whatever vast geological upheaval had produced the hills must of been one of incredible violence. There was not a single square foot of ground that Quill could see that was free of cracks and crevasses, or not covered in jagged chunks of rock. The debris spilled out onto the plain for a considerable distance, probably a day or two's walk. Quill cursed quietly, yet vehemently, under his breath. He'd hoped for a nice open space on which to land and set up camp, but there was nothing at all. Even if the beasts could land below, it would be rough on the riders.

It was on their third circle of the hills that Ansari spotted what must have been the only flat patch of ground for miles, nestled between two of the smaller hills. She gestured to the other riders and they slowly descended in ever decreasing circles. They took turns landing, the beasts far less graceful returning to the ground than they were in the air, coming down in a tangle of legs and wings, yet somehow managing to come to a halt all in one piece and upright—and with the same true of their riders. Within ten minutes they were all lined up on the edge of the clearing, and the travelers were unloading their belongings.

"Any ideas on where to go from here, Gamora?" Quill asked.

"I have no idea, to be honest," she replied. "I didn't see a single sign of life the whole time we were in the air. Did anyone else notice anything? Buildings? Campfires? Anything?"

Ansari and Quill shook their heads.

"Then the only real choice is to try and comb the hills on foot and see if we can find anything that wouldn't be visible from the air."

Quill's shoulders slumped. "That could take weeks, and we don't have that sort of time on our side."

"Well, let's hope we get lucky."

As she turned to grab her pack, there was a deep, low rumbling noise from beneath their feet. She took one more step and then leaped back like a cat as the ground opened up beneath her, only just avoiding falling into the three-foot-wide crack that had suddenly appeared. All across the clearing the ground shifted and moved, chasms yawning open then slamming shut as if the earth were hungry—and would chew them up and spit them out given half a chance. The noise and motion was too much for the beasts and they began to panic, letting out bellows of alarm and flapping their great wings. Wind from their passage through the air was enough to buffet Ansari, sending her reeling towards one of the cracks. Quill barely managed to catch her arm and pull her from harm's way.

By the time he had Ansari steady on her feet and had turned back to the beasts, they were beyond calming down, and in a frenzied flurry of wings launched themselves into the air. The tip of one of their wings caught Quill with a glancing blow, knocking him to the ground and ruining any chance of him grabbing the dangling straps and catching at least one of the beasts before it could escape. He could only watch in despair as they dwindled into the distance, taking with them any chance that remained of making his agreed upon rendezvous with the Duke. Before he could sink into too great a despondence, he was jarred by a stirring in one of the cracks that had stayed open longer than the others.

"Gamora! Ansari! Watch your backs!"

The words had barely left his mouth before the crack

seemed to explode with creatures. They were head-and-shoulders taller than Quill, and completely insectile in appearance. A chitinous shell covered their bodies, and while they stood on two segmented legs, they had an extra set of arms underneath their primary ones. These arms were thinner, with razor-sharp edges that culminated in a wicked looking point. The larger set of arms were as thick as Quill's legs, and instead of a point ended in clawlike hands, with one large finger and a commensurately-sized opposable thumb. Their heads were dominated by two faceted eyes the size of grapefruit and chittering mandibles that gnashed and moved as they emitted a high-pitched warbling that set Quill's teeth on edge.

By the time the insectoids stopped emerging from the crack in the ground, there were at least a dozen surrounding the three travelers, who stood back to back, waiting for the inevitable assault. Quill had replaced the axe handle Gamora had cracked with a short fighting staff he had found at the monastery, and Gamora was armed with two daggers as long as her forearm, holding them in a low, deadly stance. Ansari's weapon of choice was a sickle with a chain attached, weighted down at the other end with a fist-sized ball of steel. She held the sickle in one hand while twirling the weighted chain with the other, and while she looked pale, Quill had no doubt that when the time came she would be formidable indeed.

As if some inaudible signal had flashed between them, the insectoids launched themselves at the companions as one. Strangely, they all kept their secondary arms folded up against their bodies, relying on their hands as weapons. Even when the first one fell with one of Gamora's knives buried in its thorax, they refused to press the attack with their slashing limbs.

"Why are they holding back?" Gamora yelled breathlessly as she retrieved her knife, wiping green ichor from the blade. "They could have had us by now."

Quill only shrugged; he was too busy defending himself, each blow of the thick stave leaving dents in his attackers' shells. But the insectoids seemed undeterred, and he wondered whether they were even capable of feeling pain. That was the problem with fighting other species—having to guess the physiological differences. It was embarrassing kicking someone in the nuts only to discover you'd merely succeeded in giving them a bloody nose. The gripping arm of the insectoids was very good at trapping their weapons, and Quill nearly lost his stave before he cursed and gave it a good wrench. He didn't relish the thought of going up against them empty handed.

He could see Ansari was giving a good account of herself beside him. She was using the sickle to trap blows rather than to slash at the insectoids, then yanked the chain and relied on centrifugal force to send the weight crashing into her opponent with far more power than she could have generated on her own.

"She must have had a good teacher," he yelled to Gamora.

"Flatterer," she scoffed, but she was smiling.

There was no more time for talking as the insectoids redoubled their attack. It had become clear that they were going out of their way not to kill the travelers, pulling blows that would have shattered bone and refraining from deploying their slashing arms. Even with this advantage, the sheer weight of their numbers was starting to take its toll. A scream rang out across the clearing, and Quill's head whipped around just in time to see Ansari, held fast by two of the insectoids, being bundled away towards the crack. Before he could fight his way towards her, she was gone.

"Gamora, we have to go after her!" There was no answer besides a muffled groan, and he turned to see Gamora slumping to the ground, one of the insectoids standing over her with its fist still raised. "Gamora!"

As he reached for her, powerful arms grabbed him from behind. He struggled against the viselike grip, but more insectoids piled on him, wrapping him up in their implacable hold. He was lifted from his feet and flipped over an insectoid's shoulder, and he felt a wave of disorientation as the ground rushed past a few inches from his face. There was a sickening lurch as he was carried down into the chasm, his captors sure footed despite the crumbling sides. The fissure soon gave way to a broad tunnel that descended on a gentle incline, the walls smooth and polished, and covered in a glowing fungus that illuminated their way with an eerie, greenish light.

Their path was intersected regularly by other tunnels, and sometimes they would continue straight through, or turn left or right with no apparent pattern. It was not long before Quill had lost any sense of what direction they were moving in, and he fought down bouts of dizziness and claustrophobia. All he knew was that they were moving deeper and deeper, and he was far too conscious of the weight of a thousand tons of rock pressing down from above.

Occasionally, they would cross paths with another group of insectoids going about their own mysterious errands. From his awkward position it was hard for Quill to get a good look at them, but some looked identical to Quill's captors, while others varied considerably. There were groups that Quill assumed must be workers as, instead of the slashing secondary arms, they possessed another set of powerful gripping limbs. One group was made up entirely of spindly albinos; another had iridescent wings. At some of the intersections, large friezes had been chiseled into the rock, and the similarity to the designs he had seen in the cavern on the mountaintop made Quill wonder whether these were the descendants of the race that had tamed the winged beasts.

Despite its burden, the insectoid carrying Quill maintained an unflagging pace. Every five hundred feet or so, some thoughtful designer had set elegant water fountains into the walls, but there was no stopping, and Quill tried not to think about how thirsty he was. Instead, he focused on trying to assess the situation. He was conscious of being surrounded, but the way he was held meant that he could only look forward, and even that was at the price of a terrible ache in his neck. He knew that his companions were nearby, but for all he knew they might be dead or badly injured, simply more meat being taken to the creatures' larder. So, he felt a huge wave of relief when a voice hissed his name.

"Quill, are you awake?" It was Gamora, and she sounded furious. "Quill?"

"Yeah, I'm awake," he said. "Are you hurt?"

"My head is pounding, but give me a few hours' sleep and I'll be fine," she replied. "You?"

"Nothing injured but my pride," Quill said. "This is not a very dignified method of transportation."

"Forget about that for the moment. How are we going to get out of this?"

"We'll think of something," Quill said with an air of confidence he didn't really feel. "Any sign of Ansari?"

"She's about three feet behind you. She is unconscious— but she is still breathing," Gamora said. "She went down fighting and one of them knocked her over the head to keep her quiet. She's young and resilient, though."

Their conversation trailed off as the tunnel came to an end and they came out into a huge open space. It looked like a naturally-occurring cavern—stalactites made their inexorable way towards the floor, and the roof—perhaps a hundred feet above him—was rough and pitted. The only sign of artifice was the raised dais in the center of the chamber. It was surrounded by low benches, and their arrangement served to focus the eye on the throne that sat in the middle of the platform. The throne was carved from a single chunk of black obsidian, which caught the light from the fungus that covered the walls here as it had in the passageways, reflecting it and giving everything an otherworldly air.

A huge and brooding figure sat on the throne, chin resting on its fist as it regarded the prisoners who had been dumped unceremoniously before it. It was not insectile at all, and while perhaps it would not have been as tall as them if standing, its massive frame spoke of terrible and irresistible strength. Quill felt a thrill of recognition as it raised its head and met his gaze.

"So, Star-Lord, it seems fate has bought us together once more. What brings you to my realm?" Drax asked.

CHAPTER 12

"Your realm?" Quill repeated. "I'm sure there's a story in that. How did you end up ruler here?"

Drax gestured, and the humans were lifted to their feet by the servitors and sat gently on the benches—though they had to lay Ansari down on a bench of her own as she was still unconscious. A trio of the spindly insectoids Quill had seen earlier scuttled off and soon returned bearing goblets of water and nectar, as well as a tray of some unidentifiable goop that was surprisingly tasty.

"After we parted ways, I decided I needed to spend some time away from the easy life we had been living," Drax said. "I was growing weak, soft. I wandered until I came to the barren lands, living off rodents that I killed myself."

"Sounds awful," Gamora said.

"It was wonderful," Drax said, his eyes lighting up. "I felt alive. I had rediscovered the way of life that had made me so strong."

Quill and Gamora looked at each other, but didn't say a word.

"I continued my wanderings and finally I found myself in the hills. I made camp and closed my eyes. When I awoke I was surrounded by these creatures. I fought them off for as long as I could. It was a glorious battle that went on for many hours, but there were too many even for me, and as the sun peeked over the horizon I found myself carried here, like you. And like you I was dumped before the throne of their king."

Drax's story was interrupted by a moan from Ansari as she sat up, rubbing her head.

"What happened?" she groaned. "Where are we?"

Her eyes widened as she took in their surroundings, flinching away from the insectoids before stopping to stare at Drax.

"And who is he?"

"It's okay," Gamora said soothingly. "This is the friend I told you about, the one we have been searching for. Drax, this is my apprentice, Ansari."

"Greetings, apprentice of Gamora. You look weak and fragile to me, but I trust her warrior's instinct and assume you must be capable."

"Ah, thanks, I guess," Ansari said, then leaned over and whispered to Quill and Gamora. "Is he always like this?"

"Pretty much," Quill said. "Tact is not really his strong point."

More of the servitors brought Ansari some refreshments. She set to them with gusto as Drax continued with his story.

"I was meant to be an offering to the king. These creatures believe that they absorb the qualities of any living thing that they eat, and their ruler gets first choice of any sentient being. They had seen the way that I fought and believed that I was worthy to be absorbed by their ruler."

Quill couldn't help himself and started to laugh. The others looked at him quizzically.

"Stupid joke, but talk about biting off more than you can chew."

Drax ignored him and kept on talking.

"To satisfy custom, the king was expected to defeat me in single combat. When he failed, I took his place," Drax said summarily. "Well, once they cleaned the blood off the throne, anyway."

A terrible thought occurred to Quill.

"You didn't . . . eat him, did you?"

Drax looked almost comically surprised.

"What? No! He is now my best scout," Drax said. "He fought with honor, and I accorded him the respect I felt he deserved. What sort of barbarian do you take me for?"

"I don't know what I was thinking," Quill said. "I hope you can forgive me."

Drax missed the sarcasm as always.

"Apology accepted. I had no desire to be king, but it would have been disrespectful to their customs to refuse, and I would not dishonor them in that way." Drax sighed. "And now I have to rule here until someone defeats me in turn."

"Have any tried?" Gamora asked.

"Thirty-seven so far. I have attempted to be gracious and have killed only twenty of them, and that was because they gave me no choice."

"You are a benevolent king," Quill said. "No doubt about it."

"Thank you. So, now you know my story. What brings you here?"

Quill ran Drax through the situation, explaining what he had been up to since they had parted ways, and letting Gamora and Ansari tell their own parts in the tale. Finally, he explained the mission he had accepted from the Duke.

"I came searching for my friends, hoping that you might be able to help me discover the secret behind this new nomad strength. And now I discover that you are a king." He hesitated for a moment, then went on. "I am sure the Duke would welcome an alliance and be grateful for any help you could provide. You seem to have no shortage of formidable fighters."

Drax frowned, and steepled his fingers under his chin.

"It is true that we are friends, and we have been through a great deal together. I haven't forgotten the harsh words at the ship, but what's that compared to having saved each other's lives a score or more times?" Drax asked. "But I take my responsibilities as king very seriously. It is not right for me to send my subjects off to war simply because of my selfish attachments."

Quill wasn't surprised. He couldn't imagine Drax taking anything lightly, especially when it touched on his sense of honor.

"Will *you* come with us, though?" Gamora asked. "You aren't risking anyone else that way."

For a moment Quill thought Drax was going to say yes, but then he shook his head.

"It wouldn't be right to abandon my realm," Drax said. "There is no honor in disrespecting its customs, so I am bound to stay here until I am defeated in single combat."

"I understand," Quill said. The funny thing was that he actually thought he *did*. He guessed he must have spent too much time with the Destroyer and absorbed some of his notions of honor.

"I can do something for you, though," Drax said. "For the sake of our friendship, I will ensure you have safe conduct to wherever you want to go. Your mounts have been captured and they will be returned to you, along with your belongings."

As he finished, one of the insectoids began to gesticulate wildly, all four of its arms waving above its head. It was one of the warrior class that had captured them, but decidedly bigger than the others they had seen so far, broader through the shoulders and with a larger set of lashing arms. Its mandibles clashed as it chittered loudly, giving the impression of being less than happy. Drax's expression grew stonier as he listened, and Quill could see a vein pulsing at his temple.

"What's his problem?" Quill asked.

"He doesn't agree with my verdict."

"They can understand you?" Gamora asked curiously.

"Yes," Drax said. "They have a form of low-level telepathy."

"They can read minds?" Quill asked in alarm. He recalled all the uncharitable things he had thought on the way down from the surface.

"Not exactly," Drax said. "Verbalizing your thoughts lets them capture the meaning because it forces your mind to shape your thoughts into patterns that they can read, so he knows I plan on giving you safe conduct."

"What does he want to do with us instead?" Ansari asked.

Drax looked at her like she was stupid.

"Eat you, of course. What else?"

"Of course," Quill muttered. "Well, I appreciate the fact you don't share their . . . appetites. I assume you aren't going to give him what he wants?"

"No, I'm not," Drax said.

This provoked another burst of insectile invective, and Drax leaped to his feet, the waves of menace that roiled off him making even Quill take a step back.

"So, you are challenging me?" The insectile creature chittered back a response, and Drax smiled. "So be it."

With another gesture, Drax had the servitors clear away the benches. Still more servitors scattered sand across the floor and used a stick to draw a large circle about twenty paces across. Drax strode into the middle of the ring and stood waiting. He moved his head from side to side with a popping of joints, and then began to stretch and flex, working his way through every part of his body. He held up his arms and clenched his fists, the sound of knuckles cracking clearly audible. By the time he was finished, every muscle on his body stood out, clearly defined and bulging. Quill was terrified at the sight and he was standing twenty feet away—he could only imagine the effect up close.

"So, blades or no blades?" Drax asked the insectoid as it joined him in the ring. Its only response was to fold its slashing arms in against its sides and out of the way. Quill thought it was stupid; if he'd been getting in the ring with Drax he would have wanted every possible advantage—he'd take a bazooka in there if it were allowed.

Drax nodded. "So be it." He turned towards the humans. "Perhaps today is the day I am defeated and freed to go my own way. If so, I will join you. Provided I am not eaten by the victor."

He bowed to his opponent and dropped into a fighting stance. They slowly circled each other, and then the insectoid moved in on Drax. Its primary arms gave it a reach even greater than the Destroyer's and it used that to great effect, throwing punch after punch and then dancing back out of reach of Drax's counter attacks. At no time did it make any attempt to use its slashing arms, instead relying on the terrible power of its fists. Drax blocked most of its blows, but those that landed made a sickening noise, leaving Quill wincing in sympathy. Drax took the first couple of blows without any sign that they had hurt, but as he threw a punch of his own he slipped on the sand, leaving himself vulnerable to a brutal uppercut that hit him right on the point of his chin.

Drax staggered backwards, his heel coming perilously close to the line in the sand. Quill had no idea what would have happened had Drax crossed the line, but he was sure it wasn't good. The Destroyer found his balance just in time and threw himself at the insectoid. Now it was his opponent that fell back under the onslaught as Drax landed punch after punch. The creature's armor took on a rather dented appearance, and in some places the chitin had cracked completely and was leaking a green ichor that added an ammoniac reek to the air. The insectoid staggered back, and then stood, rocking on its feet. Drax drew back his fist, huge muscles bunching under the skin of his arm, but then reached out and gently pushed. Without a sound the insectoid toppled backwards and lay motionless on the ground, only the slight movement of its chest showing it still lived.

Draw took a deep breath, and looked around at the gathered insectoids.

"Does anyone else disagree with my decree?" he asked, his voice loud enough to echo from the roof of the cavern. "Anyone? Step forward now and challenge me now, or not at all."

Not a single antenna twitched, nor a mandible clicked, as every insectoid stood absolutely still. Quill would have done the same in their place.

"Excellent," Drax said. "Then it is resolved."

He turned to the humans. "You are welcome to enjoy my hospitality for a few days. There is no need to leave now."

Quill looked at Gamora and raised an eyebrow, and she nodded slightly.

"It's a very generous offer, Drax," Quill said. "But time is running out, so if it's all the same to you, I think we should hit the road."

"As you wish," Drax said. "I commend your dedication. I will have you taken to your mounts and given as many provisions as you can take with you. I hope this helps."

"It helps a lot, Drax," Gamora said. "Thank you."

She reached into Quill's saddlebag and pulled out his map, then walked over to Drax.

"Humor me, though. I am not saying you will, but just in case you do change you mind, let me show you where we plan on meeting the Duke." She placed a hand on Drax's shoulder and led him towards one of the tables. She laid the map out and began to trace lines with her finger. "From here, you would take this road and meet us here."

Drax laughed. "If I did decide to join you, I have a much quicker way of traveling. The tunnels extend much farther than you would expect. If it weren't for your flying beasts I would send you that way." He turned away from the table and walked towards his throne. "But it is inconsequential. I have spoken."

While Gamora and Drax had been conferring, the servitors had been busy retrieving all of the companions' belongings and putting together bundles of provisions. As soon as the travelers' saddlebags were full, they were loaded onto the backs of servitors and a company of the insectoid soldiers formed up around them.

"Farewell, my friends," Drax said. "I wish you glory and honor in your coming battles."

Quill raised his hand in a casual salute, and then followed the insectoids out of the cavern. The journey was much more pleasant this time around, which probably had something to do with the fact that Quill was moving under his own power and not hanging upside down. They took a different set of tunnels, curving slightly to the left and climbing steadily. Quill soon realized that they were being taken to the top of the hill in which the nest rested, the tunnel corkscrewing around the outside of it. As they progressed, the solid walls began to feature wide, low windows that looked out over the desolate plains. It wasn't much of a view, but the sunshine and fresh air was a welcome change after the dark closeness of the tunnels below. By the time they emerged blinking onto the flattened top of the hill, Quill was starting to feel like his old self, and had even munched on some of the provisions they had been given. The fungus wasn't actually that bad—if you were hungry enough.

As promised, their mounts were waiting for them. Quill had no idea how the insectoids had managed to recapture them, but he suspected that his inkling of a link between them and the race that had tamed the beasts might not be too far from the truth. Whatever the case, he was duly grateful—with their steeds they had a real chance of making the rendezvous on time. Not that he relished the idea of telling the Duke that so far, he had not only failed to discover anything more about the enemy, but had only bought him two warriors and some flying animals. As they ascended, Quill tried to put such thoughts from his mind. The wind streaming through his hair and the sight of the insectoids dwindling beneath him on the ground were experiences to be savored. He could deal with his worries when the time came, but for now he was going to enjoy what fleeting pleasures came his way.

CHAPTER 13

"So, what do you think of them? I want your professional opinion—don't hold back."

Quill took his time answering, trying to work out the right way to phrase what he had to say. Things were . . . delicate with the Duke. There hadn't been a scene when Quill had joined the army's march without any new intelligence—no threats of execution or banishment, and there had been no objections to him taking his place on the Duke's council. In fact, his first morning back he had been woken far too early by a spotty-faced page and summoned to a meeting. Quill had expected to be facing a hostile reception—perhaps even a tribunal—but instead the Duke and his advisors had simply made him part of the discussion about the disposition of forces and military tactics.

Despite all that, there was a coldness in the way the Duke spoke to him that had never been there before. He was scrupulously polite, nothing in what he said or how he acted that Quill could broach with him, but it was not the same. Quill wasn't sure whether it was that the Duke had found out about his relationship with Karyn, or simply that he felt Quill had failed him—and in fairness, Quill knew that he had failed—but in either case, Quill was very conscious of treading carefully around him. When the Duke had asked him to come along for an inspection of the army, Quill had eagerly agreed. It was a lovely day for riding, the sun shining, oblivious to the carnage and suffering that would unfold over the next few days, warming the wicked and the righteous alike.

"Well?" the Duke asked, the first notes of impatience appearing in his voice.

"Sire, these are good troops, there is no doubt about it. The core of seasoned veterans you have built are of the highest quality, and the levies you have called up seem to be solid men. I am especially impressed with how well equipped they are; you haven't stinted. A lot of civilian levies only carry what weapons they can find or, more likely, they carry farm tools."

"But?" the Duke asked. "I can hear that there is one."

"Sire, they aren't ready. You have the makings of an army here, a very good army. But right now, all they are is a group of men marching in the same direction," Quill said. "The levies don't understand half the commands they're given, and the veterans don't see comrades, just farmers. They need time to train together, to come together as a cohesive group."

"You might be right, Lord Quill, but time is the one thing we don't have. I have men, and I have a surplus of equipment and supplies. I need to use my strengths such as they are."

"Sire, meaning no disrespect, I don't understand what the hurry is. Even a few weeks could make all the difference here."

The Duke sighed, and for a moment Quill could see all of the Duke's years weighing heavily on him.

"Lord Quill, whatever your failings, I have the utmost respect for your military experience and knowledge. But this is about something more—it is about politics," the Duke almost spat the word, "and about what it is to be a leader."

Quill said nothing, but waited for the Duke to continue.

"The Empire is at a tipping point. The Emperor is only a boy, and his Regent is one of the city's faction of nobles. As far as they are concerned, there is nothing of importance outside of the capital. We country nobles do what we can to counteract their influence, but having the Emperor's ear is a huge advantage for them when it comes to power games. It's bad enough that one of our faction failed to stop the invasion. Gods curse them, the city nobles will already be making political capital from that. I can't believe that the combined forces of the Empire won't be able to stop this army—what you see here is only a fraction of the troops that they command— but if I am unable to stem the invasion before it reaches the capital, it will only reinforce their view of our worth. It will make things far, far worse, and we may lose what independence we have. It's not only that it will be bad for us—I have never sought my own gain above the good of the realm—but that it will be bad for the Empire. Too many of our subjects live outside the capital. They deserve to be championed, too, and the city nobles would rather forget they exist."

"I see, sire," Quill said. He did see, but he wasn't sure it was quite that simple, or that the Duke was not underestimating the danger the invaders posed. "But would a few weeks or months really be held against you if you could demonstrate their necessity for victory?"

"That's the second part, Lord Quill. Leadership is not about privilege; it is about responsibility. The people of the Empire trust their rulers to protect them. It is part of the contract that we have with them. Every soldier who has died—or every civilian—is someone whom we have let down; that we have failed. Every day that the nomads occupy our duchies, more will die, and each life matters," the Duke said. "And the nomads won't stay in one place for long—it's not in their nature. They will continue towards the heart of the Empire, and as they get closer, more lives will be lost. The frontier duchies are less populated and, more importantly, accustomed to invasions. As the nomads get closer to the capital, the towns have weaker walls and there are more concentrated populations with nowhere to flee. It will be a red slaughter, day in and day out. The nomads have to be stopped before that happens."

"I'm sorry I doubted you, sire," Quill said, giving a slight bow of his head. "We will just have to do the best we can with what we have."

"Lord Quill, telling me what you really think is not something you ever need to be sorry for. I have plenty of men who will tell me exactly what I want to hear."

Quill laughed. "Sire, I have a friend that I hope you get to meet in person one day. I think you'd find you have a lot in common—from ideas about leadership to the importance of speaking your mind. My friend Drax is incapable of holding back."

They continued to inspect the army. The veterans were mainly infantry, armed with short, stabbing swords and tall shields, but Quill was relieved to see around five hundred heavy cavalry, as well as twice as many light cavalry. He nodded in approval—the light cavalry would be able to act as a screen, while if given the opportunity, the heavy cavalry would ride over anything that got in its path. The levies, however, were a bit of a mix. There were a number of companies of archers armed with longbows that Quill liked the look of. Their range would come in very handy, especially at the beginning of the battle to harry the nomads as they approached, and rain down death upon them during their charge. The rest were mostly pikemen who also carried short swords for close-in fighting. Quill had mixed feelings about this group—on the one hand it didn't take much training to use a pike, but on the other hand, the most important quality in a pikeman was the willingness to stand firm in the face of a charge. The levies were untested, and none—not even the levies themselves—knew how it would go when it came time to hold their positions in the face of the enemy.

There were also a few specialist companies. Some were

engineers, responsible for everything from building forti-fications as needed to building bridges. There was also an artillery company, armed with ballistae and trebuchets. The trebuchets were the most advanced piece of machinery Quill had seen among the Empire's arsenal since landing on the planet, and for a moment he wondered why none of the civilizations he had encountered had progressed beyond a certain point. Quill remembered the smashed computer in the village on the mountain and the hints scattered all over the countryside of an older civilization—or many—that had mysteriously disappeared. He wondered what had happened to the creatures that had produced the calculating machine, and why the most advanced civilization of the present hadn't even gotten to the steam engine. The Duke was staring at him impatiently, and Quill pulled his thoughts back to the matter at hand.

According to the Duke's scribes, the army was made up of just over four thousand men, almost half of whom were veterans, making it only slightly bigger than what the scouts claimed the nomads had been able to muster. Quill would have preferred to have a much larger advantage, knowing that it took a lot of troops to make up for an enemy pos-sessing superior tactics or technology. Quill frowned at the reminder that there was still the unknown quantity of the shadowy riders to deal with. He had no idea how many men they were worth. His only consolation was that the first army to face the nomads had held its own for at least the first part of the battle, and it had only been half the size of the one the Duke had put together.

"Sire, what happens if we are unable to stop them?"

The Duke seemed about to reply with anger, then visibly calmed himself.

"I suppose that's a fair question," he said, smiling slightly. "I am, of course, operating on the assumption that we will be victorious—to do anything less would be admitting defeat before we even march. But, if we aren't, hopefully it will shock the Regent into action before they reach the capital's walls. He can call on far more resources than I can."

"Sire, forgive me if the idea of being part of a noble sacrifice doesn't appeal. I'd much rather win."

The Duke roared with laughter. "Me too, Lord Quill, me too. So, do you have any further thoughts on deployment or tactics?"

"A few. I'm not sure our winged beasts can carry enough rocks to do any real damage, but we can cause some problems for the enemy," Quill said. "More importantly, it will be great for reconnaissance. Air power is a game changer."

"I think you just made your journey worthwhile, Lord Quill," the Duke said, his tone the warmest it had been since Quill had returned. "Any other suggestions?"

"Yes, sire. The nomads fight on horseback using those repeating bows, and are lightly armored and fast." The Duke nodded. "We need to be careful not to fall into the trap of fighting on their terms."

"What do you mean?" the Duke asked.

"They will either try to draw us out and cut us to pieces, or dart in and out of range and pepper us with arrows," Quill explained, "like a little dog nipping at a big one."

"So what do we do about it?"

"As we approach, you should use your light cavalry as a screen to stop the nomads from harassing your flanks. You need shield men on either side of the column, and with the warning your light cavalry gives, they can keep the arrows off of us." Quill dismounted and began to draw pictures in the dirt. "When we get close enough to the nomads' main force, we need to pick the right terrain and wait for them to come to us. You'll want a mixed force at the front, veterans to form a shield wall mixed with pikemen, and then the archers behind them."

"Why the mix?" the Duke asked.

"The nomads will attempt to break your front line with their damn archery. Given the reported range of their bows, the shield wall will stop that, and the longbows will be able to rain death upon them and force them to charge—they'll have to get in among your men so you can't use your bows for fear of hitting your own. Then the pikes will stop the charge, as long as the levies stand firm," Quill said. "This is where you want good terrain with some cover to either side. I'd split my heavy cavalry in two, and try and hide them to both the left and right. While the nomads are engaged with your infantry, the heavy cavalry will hit them from both sides—the hammer and the anvil. If they try and escape to the front, they run into the pikes, and if they retreat, your archers come back into play. The trebuchets and ballistae will supplement the archers quite nicely, too."

"I like the sound of that plan, Lord Quill," the Duke said.

"So do I, sire, but they say that plans only survive until contact with the enemy." Quill straightened up and brushed the dust from his knees. "I do think that this is our best option, and all things being equal, I like our chances."

Quill grabbed his horse's reins, and in one swift motion mounted it.

"The important thing is, sire, that we can't lose our heads. If we pursue too aggressively, or allow the nomads to draw us out of formation, they will cut us to pieces. We can't compete with their mobility."

"Excellent work, Lord Quill. I will call a meeting tonight with all of the commanders, and you can present this to them."

"Wouldn't it be better coming from you, sire?" Quill asked.

"Don't worry, I will impress upon them the need to listen to you as if the words are my own. Anyone who fails to do so will answer to me," the Duke said. "And on the day of the battle I will require you in the command tent. Marius will have overall command, but he is not the sort of man who would ignore an advisor of your experience—especially once he sees your planning."

"And where will you be, sire?" Quill asked. "The command tent?"

"No, I trust Marius, and my presence would only undermine him. I will be doing my duty, ensuring that I am seen in my armor." He laughed at the look of horror on Quill's face. "I will not be going anywhere near the front line. I have nothing to prove, and I won't be leading any charges. If I were to fall, it would have too detrimental an effect on morale. But seeing me riding up and down the lines should hearten the men."

"It sounds like you have it all worked out, sire," Quill said.

"As much as is possible, Lord Quill," the Duke replied. "Now the only thing left to do is fight."

"Not quite, sire," Quill said. At the Duke's questioning look he went on. "The only thing left to do is *win*."

CHAPTER 14

For an army that hadn't existed even a few weeks before, the Duke's forces made very good time. Quill supposed that the farmers and foresters were used to working from sunrise to sunset, and probably saw this as a respite from their usual backbreaking labor—at least until the fighting started. Still, Quill was impressed—they kept up with the veterans, ensuring that there was no resentment from them at being slowed down. For a culture that avoided out-and-out warfare, the Empire had a strong military tradition. It was only internal conflict that was solved by the system of champions that had given Quill his place in society. There were constant skirmishes with the nomads to the east, and Quill learned that there was a loose confederation of city states to the north of the Empire with whom they occasionally came into conflict as well.

The Empire had set up an academy to train commanders who were expected to serve in one of these hot spots or on the vast inland sea, chasing pirates. This meant that there was a solid core of experienced commanders to call upon in the rare times that mass mobilization was needed. While many had died at the beginning of the nomad invasion during the fall of Astarlia, they had only been one part of the Empire's resources. Quill had been impressed by the commanders—when he had presented his plans, there had been none of the usual arguing for arguing's sake, or the fear of anything new that he had come to expect from military minds. Instead, he had been asked a series of probing questions that went straight to the heart of the plan, and had been given some suggestions that had refined and improved his original ideas.

Quill, Gamora, and Ansari had been kept busy flying reconnaissance flights. They had already prevented a number of casualties when they had been able to warn the army before it stumbled into a large force of nomads that had gone ahead of the main army in search of fresh spoils. Instead, the nomads had been surrounded and wiped out, a much-needed victory that had raised morale and stiffened the spines of the untested levies. Quill was much more confident that they would stand firm now; there was nothing like the taste of victory to create self-confidence. He knew that the real test still lay ahead, and it would be a much tougher battle than this one—but he was happy to take whatever advantages he could find.

Every night, the soldiers would drill before they were allowed to eat, and then endured another round of practice after their meal. There had been some grumbling to start with, but after that first battle it seemed like the soldiers had realized the importance of being prepared. They trained in their own specialties separately before joining each other for joint exercises. Quill had been pleasantly surprised by how the veterans had embraced the levies, but he guessed it was probably the universal pragmatism of the career soldier at work. It was in their best interest to make sure that the men fighting alongside them were as prepared as possible.

Gamora rode up alongside Quill, and together they watched the men train.

"I wish we had more time," she said. "If you gave me even a few months, I could turn this into a real army—and I'd back them against anyone."

Gamora had been invaluable in helping train the men. Quill was willing to admit that she was a better hand-to-hand fighter than him, and she had been raised from birth to be not only an unstoppable fighter, but a commander of troops as well. Thanos, her adoptive father and one of the most powerful beings in the galaxy, had always intended her to be one of his chief lieutenants, and yet here she was, using the skills and training he had given her to help—not destroy. Quill felt a wave of admiration for her, and not for the first time. He'd never met someone who had so completely transcended their origins.

"You're right," he said. "They are quality soldiers. And I think that when it comes to the crunch, they'll make us proud."

Suddenly there was a commotion among the picket lines, and the sound of horses whinnying with fear. Neither Quill or Gamora blinked an eye.

"That'll be Ansari returning," Gamora said.

The horses still hadn't gotten used to the flying beasts and reacted to their presence with a mix of terror and aggression. There had been an attempt at keeping them separate, but the horses could smell the flying beasts anywhere in the camp, and reacted no differently whether they could see them or not. Unfortunately, the campsite hadn't had too many flat places for the creatures to land, so they were closer than Quill would have liked. This time he knew that Ansari had important news, because she didn't even bother tethering her beast herself as she would have normally done, instead throwing the rein to a startled groomsman and running straight for Quill and Gamora. When she skidded to a halt, she was breathless.

"The nomads have started moving!" Ansari exclaimed, not even bothering with a greeting. "If we keep going the way we have been, we will meet them late tomorrow afternoon."

Quill grinned. "Ah, but we *won't* be going on the way we have been." He shouted out some orders and grabbed the page who had appeared in response. "Take this message to the Duke. Tell him it's time to implement Plan Roadhouse. Got that?"

The page nodded, and without even asking what Quill was talking about, disappeared into the camp. Not fifteen minutes later, horns rang out, and they heard the sound of men hastily gathering up their equipment.

"What's going on?" Ansari asked.

"One of the first rules of war is never to simply react to what your enemy is doing," Gamora said. "And certainly, never to be where your enemy expects you to be."

While he had used Ansari to track the location of the enemy, Quill had spent most of his time on his own reconnaissance flights scouting out the countryside between his army and the nomads. He had flagged several sites as an ideal place for their battle, and was pleased that one of the most favorable ones was with within reach. It was a broad valley with wooded slopes that would not only serve to funnel the nomads towards his front line, but would also allow him to conceal the heavy cavalry on his flanks. By the time the sun rose, the army was in place.

Quill rode up to where the Duke and his council stood overlooking the battle lines. Marius, the old warrior, looked at home, but Tremas seemed out of place in his rich furs. Still, Quill had to admire the Master of Coin—he could have stayed behind quite easily, and a man of lesser courage would have done so. Quill dismounted and moved to stand beside the Duke.

"Do you think they will walk into our trap?" the Duke asked. He was as anxious as Quill had ever seen him, crackling with nervous energy as he paced back and forth.

"Sire, nothing is certain when it comes to war," Quill said. "But I don't see what choice they have. If they go around us, they run the risk of us mounting a surprise attack on their rear, or being trapped between two forces—they don't know whether this is the only army they'll face. And the sides of the valley are too steep for them to come down upon us, which is one of the reasons why I chose it. I don't think that they have any choice but to engage us."

"What do you think, Lord Marius?" the Duke asked. Quill wasn't offended; he could see that the Duke was just seeking reassurance.

"Sire, I agree with Lord Quill. I think that this is the best opportunity we will have," the Master of Arms said. Quill nodded to him in a gesture of gratitude.

"Lord Quill is to be commended, sire." Quill stared at Tremas in surprise. The other man continued. "He may not have achieved all of the goals of the mission you sent him on, but the use of his winged beasts and Gamora's tactical skills have been invaluable."

"Thank you, Lord Tremas," Quill said.

"Don't make the mistake of thinking I like you, off-worlder," the older man snapped. "But I love the realm, and anything that serves to protect it has my approval."

Quill didn't reply. At least the Master of Coin was honest. The Duke ignored the byplay.

"I suppose that all we can do is wait."

"Often the hardest part, sire," Quill said. "We believe that the nomads will encounter our screen of light cavalry midmorning. We have at least five hours—I suggest that we let the men sleep, and that you try to as well."

By the time Quill awoke, the sun had risen completely. He could hear the sound of horns in the distance—the signal that the nomads had been sighted and that the first blows had been exchanged. He hurried to the command tent, which had been set up on the crest of a low hill. The front of the tent was open and provided an excellent view of the valley. A number of men holding flags stood to either side, clearly visible to their counterparts below. The Empire had developed a form of semaphore that would allow them to signal orders to their troops far more quickly than any runners could accomplish. It was a surprisingly efficient system. Quill looked out over the valley, blinking at the sun's reflection off of the tips of pikes and the brightly polished armor. The troops were laid out exactly as he had suggested. Behind the ranks of infantry stood row after row of archers, arrows planted point down in the ground like deadly saplings waiting to have the fruit of death plucked from them. And there, nestled among the archers, the ballistae and trebuchets waited to give the nomads the surprise of their lives. He could make out the splendid figure of the Duke, astride a white stallion and clad in the gold-chased armor of state that normally hung in his great hall, riding through them all and urging his troops on. It was a heartening sight, and Quill wondered why there was a cold thread of disquiet stirring in his mind.

He'd been so caught up in his thoughts that he started when a voice sounded in his ear.

"Well, Lord Quill, everything is in place, and each commander has his orders," Marius said. "All we can do now is stand and watch . . . and hope."

Quill could make out a cloud of dust approaching the front ranks. As neatly as even the biggest martinet could have asked, the front lines split down the middle to allow the light cavalry to find refuge, and then snapped back into place. Quill could hear trumpets blowing, and the archers moved as one to draw their bows. There was another trumpet call, and they released, filling the air with a deadly rain that arced over the front line and down into what Quill hoped was the oncoming nomads—though they were still hidden from his view. The archers kept up their fatal rhythm, flight after flight of arrows filling the air. As Quill watched, the half-dozen trebuchets joined in, sending chunks of stone as big as a horse flying through the air. Flags flashed their signals, and a junior officer ran into the command tent with their messages.

"Lords, the signals commander reports that the nomads are taking heavy casualties and appear to be preparing to charge our front lines in order to get out from under our bombardment."

"Excellent," Marius said with evident satisfaction. "It's nice when a plan comes together, eh, Lord Quill?"

Quill grinned. "I love it when it does."

Marius turned to the junior officer. "Instruct the flag men to send out the following signal. 'Proceed as planned and prepare for the anvil.'"

"Yes, sir!" The junior officer saluted and ran back to the waiting signalers.

"Now let's hope that the next stage goes as well as the last."

Down below, the first wave of the nomads had hit the front ranks of the Empire's troops. The soldiers had done exactly what they were trained to do as the men with shields protected the pikemen behind them from the deadly rain of arrows that the nomads unleashed with their repeating bows. Here and there a soldier fell, but the troops were holding up even better than Quill had dared hope. The sun glinted as the pikemen lowered their weapons, creating a glittering, deadly hedge of steel. The front line rippled as the nomad charge crashed into it—and held! Quill watched the swirling chaos as the nomads tried to hack their way through, attempting to force their way past comrades who had been impaled on pikes or dodge the flying hoofs of riderless, panicked horses. Those of the enemy who did break through found themselves beset on all sides by swordsmen who made short work of them. Some of the nomads attempted to flee but found themselves riding back into the archer's field of fire.

Whatever their other flaws, the nomads were brave men— Quill had to give them that. Whoever their commander was, he or she must have realized that their normal harrying tactics would not work, and that despite the failure of the first attempt, their best option was to break through the front ranks. The nomads formed up for another charge, this time with twice the number. As they bore down on the Empire's troops, the archers had to stop shooting lest they hit their own men.

"Now, Lord Marius, if you please!" Quill yelled.

Marius ripped off an order and the flag bearers went to work even as the nomads hit the front line again. This time it didn't just ripple but bowed in, but the troops were ready for the attack. A number of gaps formed and the ballistae rolled forward. With a twang that was audible even from where Quill stood, they unleashed hell. Each ballista was loaded with a cylindrical bundle of hundreds of arrows, and as they were propelled forward with tremendous force, they spread out. By the time the arrows reached the nomads, their area of impact had expanded to twenty or thirty feet, and within that segment the carnage was horrendous. Still, the nomads kept coming, and the ballista crews were only able to loose one or two more shots before the gaps in the line needed to close up. But they had bought enough time for the next stage in the plan to unfold.

"There!"

Marius was pointing to the right-hand slope of the valley, and the riders cascading down towards the main battle. Quill knew that they were mirrored on the other side. The heavy cavalry had been hidden in the trees and now they would take the nomads—occupied with the main line of troops—on either side. He frowned—there was something wrong with the picture in front of him. As the men around him cheered, Quill felt a sudden chill wash over him.

"Lord Marius! Signal for retreat. We need to get back into a square formation."

"Are you crazy, man?" Marius snapped. "We have them."

"Lord Marius, please! Look closely. Those aren't *our* men."

"What?" Marius leaned forward. "Gods help us all. You're right."

They had been so sure of what they were seeing that none of them had really looked—Quill included. The riders were all in black, on black horses, and it was clear that they were the shadowy figures that the survivors had described as part of the rout of the Astarlian forces. Quill realized that all of his heavy cavalrymen must be lying dead in the woods—and that he had been completely fooled. The soldiers below them were expecting the cavalry and were not paying attention to the threat on their flanks.

Marius was furiously shouting orders at the flag bearers, but it was too late. With a crash of metal that echoed across the valley, the black tide piled into the Empire's soldiers. The lines reeled at the impact, and as Quill watched, the dark figures slashed and hacked their way deep into the defenders. Here and there, pockets of men stood firm and tried to resist, but the nomads took advantage of the chaos among their enemies and launched another charge that trapped the Empire's soldiers between them and the dark figures.

"Lord Marius, you need to try and get as many of your men out of here as you can. Fall back, run—I don't care—but we must save as many soldiers as possible and retreat to the castle."

"And what will you be doing, off-worlder?" Contempt dripped from Tremas's voice. "Cutting and running. I suppose you can just fly out of here."

"I'll be flying, all right," Quill said coldly. "I'm going to retrieve the Duke. Without him, the realm may very well be doomed."

"I'm getting sick of apologizing to you, Lord Quill," Tremas said, flushing with embarrassment. "But I hope to get the chance to again when we meet back at the castle. Now go."

Quill wasted no more words and sprinted for his mount. Within minutes he was in the air and swooping over the battlefield, his eyes searching for the Duke. There! He was in the middle of a knot of his men, surrounded on all sides by nomads. Quill knew that the older man would not be able to stay out of the fight, leading from behind the lines was not his style at all. Somehow, the dark riders hadn't noticed him yet, and the veteran soldiers were holding their own—they were his elite guard, and the best troops he had. From Quill's vantage point, he could spot the moment a group of the black horsemen began to hack their way towards the Duke. Quill pulled on the reins, and his mount banked in the air and descended towards the Duke.

There was an evil, buzzing noise as a bolt streaked past his ear—the nomads had seen him and were doing their best to shoot him down. Leaning over the side of his mount, Quill braced himself just in time to grab the top of the Duke's breastplate. He screamed in pain as the sudden weight nearly pulled his arm from his shoulder socket and—much worse—almost sent his steed crashing into the ground. With a mighty effort and a furious beating of its wings, it pulled them both up into the air. Quill grunted with effort as he pulled the Duke up into position in front of him.

"No—take me back!" the Duke yelled furiously. "I will not abandon my men!"

"Sire, the battle is lost. You can best serve your men by surviving and fighting the next one."

The Duke began to struggle, his violent movements nearly tipping them both from the beast's back.

"Take me back! I command it!"

Again he tried to grab at the reins.

"You need to stop, sire."

There was a hitching beat to the creature's wings that Quill didn't like, and when he looked down at its side he saw four or five arrows buried in its flesh, green ichor dripping from the wounds. The Duke's struggles weren't helping; every time he lunged the beast would groan in pain. Quill made a quick mental calculation and sighed.

"I am sorry, sire, for what I am about to do," Quill said. "I hope you will forgive me when you wake up."

"Wake up? What are you—"

The Duke was cut off midword by Quill's fist crashing into his chin, and his eyes rolled back in his head as he slumped. Quill caught him and held him tightly as they flew towards the castle.

CHAPTER 15

Survivors of the rout had been straggling in for weeks, but the flow had slowed to a trickle, and Quill thought that they probably now had almost as many soldiers as they were going to get. It wasn't quite as bad as it had looked when the dark riders were carving their way through the Empire's army, but it was a long way from good. As far as Quill had been able to work out, they had perhaps a third of the soldiers that they had set out with, and maybe nine in ten of those were fit enough to fight. One reason for Quill to resign himself to settle for what they had, however, was that any remaining returnees would have to find a way to sneak past the army now camped on the castle's doorstep.

"Cooped up in mine own castle," the Duke said. He was standing beside Quill on the parapet, looking down at the enemy. "How did it come to this?"

The bruises had almost faded from the Duke's face, leaving only a sickly yellow tinge to show that they had ever been there. Quill hoped that the memory of the blow that had inflicted them had faded, too. When the Duke had regained consciousness, Quill had genuinely been concerned that the man was going to have a stroke. He had ranted and raved and had threatened to lock Quill in the deepest, darkest dungeon he could find and throw away the key. It had been only the unlikely intervention of Tremas that had calmed the Duke down. The Master of Coin had reminded the Duke that Quill had probably saved his life and—most importantly—the realm needed him alive, now more than ever. The Duke had finally agreed, but Quill was still treading softly.

"Sire, it's not over yet. In any siege, those inside the place besieged are in a better situation than the besiegers. All they need to do is wait, while the attackers have to force the issue against walls and whatever you can throw down on them. At least, until the food runs out, anyway."

"Lord Quill, that may be true, but how long do you honestly think we can hold out? We have hundreds of injured soldiers but few of the resources we need to treat them. We are running low on food, and have many, many civilians to feed."

"Can we expect reinforcements from the Regent, sire?" Quill asked and then, remembering Rocket's words when they had last parted, added, "I had hoped to bring you some, but I have no way of knowing when they will arrive."

He left the "if ever" unspoken.

The Duke sighed. "I wish I knew. I have sent messengers to the capital, but there is no word back. I don't know whether I am being ignored or whether my couriers are being intercepted."

"We could take one of the winged beasts. No one can intercept *them*, sire."

"I have considered that, Lord Quill, but I think not, for two reasons. First, they are one of the few advantages we have, and I am hesitant to risk throwing that away."

"And the second?" Quill asked.

"The city faction have little time for anyone from outside the capital, let alone from outside the Empire itself. To call them xenophobic would be an understatement," the Duke said. "I'm worried that if one of you turned up on one of those beasts, it would do my cause more harm than good. The sad thing is that one of my men would receive almost as short shrift. The only one they would be willing to listen to is me, and I must stay here with my people."

"I see. Politics." Quill made the word sound scatological.

"Exactly," the Duke said. "We do have one thing on our side, however. This castle was built to withstand siege. It would take months to knock down these walls, no matter how many siege engines they have. And the nomads have never been known for their artillery."

"I hate to tell you this, sire, but I think they will be from now on."

He pointed to a bustle of activity. The nomads were wheeling out vast trebuchets, twice as big as the ones that the Duke's army had been able to field. Quill counted eight of the monstrosities. The nomads arrayed them in a semi-circle facing the castle, and then began to load them.

"Sire, I think that we should find somewhere else to stand. Things look to get a little lively here."

"They aren't even close to being in range. Not even trebuchets that big can throw rocks this far."

Quill hadn't had a great deal of experience with this level of technology. The artillery he was used to could have hit the castle from the other side of the planet.

"I will take your word for it, sire."

One after the other, the trebuchets released their payloads. The two men watched as the huge rocks arced through the air, growing larger and larger to the eye as they came closer and closer. Quill wondered whether the Duke had been wrong.

"Ah, sire, are you sure about the range on those things?"

"Not as sure as I was."

"Should we find another vantage point, sire?" Quill asked, trying to sound casual.

"All right, Lord Quill, let's do that."

Before they could move, the first boulder hit the castle wall with a terrible crash. The stone shook beneath them, almost sending them to the ground. The sound of the crash was like rolling thunder as the other rocks hit, sending fragments of stone flying. There were screams of pain from some unlucky soldiers who had gotten in the way. Quill grabbed the Duke's arm and dragged him back into the keep. They could hear the sound of still more rocks hitting the walls, and the keep itself seemed to tremble beneath the impacts.

"How much of that can the walls take?" Quill asked.

"I don't know," the Duke answered. "Those rocks are far bigger than anything that the designers of the castle would have imagined. Maybe a few days, if that."

"I suppose we can't be too surprised. Better bows, better armor—and now bigger and better trebuchets," Quill said. "We need a plan that takes into account the fact that those walls are going to come down sooner rather than later."

"The plan is simple, Lord Quill," the Duke answered. "We will have to make our last stand and hope we buy enough time for the civilians to escape, and for whatever help is on its way—if any is coming—to arrive in time."

That wasn't really what Quill wanted to hear, but for the life of him, he couldn't see any other options.

"Lord Quill, there is no need for you to die here, too. If you were to take your two companions and fly away, I would understand." The Duke stopped and looked at Quill, and for the first time Quill felt that the Duke was addressing him as one man to another, rather than as a Duke to his subject. "All I would ask is that you find room for my daughter."

"Sire, I have done a lot of things in my life I'm not proud off. I've stolen, I've lied, and I may even have chased one or two women. But I have never abandoned my friends. I don't run away from people who need me," Quill said. "Your daughter can take one of the beasts, but I won't be going with her."

The Duke reached out and clasped his hand.

"Thank you, Lord Quill."

The rest of the day dragged, and as Quill went about his business, it was punctuated by the pounding of rocks on the walls. He had returned to the Duke's chamber when the endgame began.

There was a sudden crash—far louder than any of the others that had gone before—and then the sound of footsteps as someone ran into the chamber.

"Sire, the walls are breached!"

The speaker was a young guard, hair plastered with sweat and blood, and with a look of panic on his face.

"Have the summons blown, and have every man who is not already on the walls and can hold a sword gather in the courtyard. Now!"

"Yes, sire!" The guard saluted and ran back the way he had come.

"Well, Lord Quill, looks like it is time for that last stand."

By the time they had made their way to the top of the wall, the fighting had started. The breach was not huge, about the size of one of the gates, but the nomads had decided to force the issue and were streaming towards it. The upside was that the bombardment had stopped—the nomads were not so mad with bloodlust as to relish crushing their own men. Or perhaps it was simply that the nomads had run out of ammunition. Boulders that size couldn't have been that easy to come by, and a good thing, too. If Quill had been in charge, he wouldn't have ordered the charge until his ammunition was depleted, but would have continued to pound the castle with boulders until it was a pile of rubble. Whatever the reason, he wasn't going to look a gift horse in the mouth.

The breach in the wall provided a bottleneck that limited the nomads' sheer numerical advantage and allowed the Duke's soldiers to hold them back. Archers stood on the walls to either side and poured arrows down into the milling mass of the enemy. At that range there was no need to even aim, and with every arrow a nomad fell screaming—or silent—in death. Despite the flow of the battle going with the defenders for the moment, Quill was under no illusions. They were outnumbered far too heavily for their fortune to continue. Even if they killed three nomads for every defender who fell, it would still be the nomads left standing at the end of the day. But at least the Vylarans would go down fighting.

Yelling from farther down the wall alerted Quill to a new problem. The nomads hadn't just stopped at trebuchets, it seemed. Scaling ladders now touched the parapets in a dozen places, and the first nomads were coming over the top. Looking around, Quill realized that he would have to do something about it himself. Raising his sword, he charged at the first of the nomads, ducking under the man's wild swing and shouldering him over the edge. He paused to push the first ladder away from the wall, watching with satisfaction as it toppled to the ground, complete with screaming nomads. By now some of the Duke's soldiers had joined him, and they fought their way along the wall, dealing with ladders and nomads alike. Ahead of him, Quill could see more soldiers doing the same, and together they somehow managed to keep the enemy from gaining a foothold on the wall.

As the last ladder crashed into splinters on the ground below, Quill took the opportunity to catch his breath. Just as he was starting to feel better, however, he saw something that made him feel sick. The Duke had entered the fighting in the courtyard, and was in the thick of it. Quill hurried down the surviving steps, leaping across the gaps that had appeared when the wall had collapsed. He nearly fell backwards into one particularly broad one, only saving himself with a frantic windmilling of his arms. He rushed into the courtyard, slashing his way through any nomad stupid enough to get in his way.

"Sire!" Quill gasped as him came up alongside the Duke. "What are you doing?"

"What does it look like? I am defending my castle!" the Duke exclaimed. Blood ran down his face from a shallow cut just under his eye, but there was much more blood on his sword.

"You shouldn't be out here," Quill said. "You should be back in the castle."

"Why?"

The Duke's eyes flashed with such anger that Quill nearly took a step back, but instead ducked as the Duke's sword came whistling towards his head. Quill was about to react defensively when he heard a terrible gurgle from behind him, and turned just in time to see a nomad slump to the ground.

"Were you going to say I am too old, perhaps?" the Duke asked. "Or too slow?"

"I was going to say too *important*, sire, but I am scared to say anything now," Quill said with a wry grin.

"I appreciate you concern, but it doesn't matter whether it is here or hiding in the keep—we are all going to die today," the Duke said. "All I can do is choose to die well."

"Fair enough," Quill said. "I can't argue with that. But I wanted to tell you something. It took a lot of persuading—and I mean a lot—but I convinced Gamora to take Ansari and Karyn back to the monastery. Karyn wanted to stay and fight—all of them did. Actually, your daughter had to be restrained to get her on the back of the beast."

"That's my girl," the Duke said proudly.

"They'll be safe enough there—safer than anywhere else I can think of."

The Duke put a hand on Quill's shoulder, and squeezed.

"Thank you, Lord Quill. I can die now knowing my child will survive."

Quill and the Duke stood back to back, desperately fighting off their attackers. The bodies of the enemy piled up at their feet, but for each nomad they cut down, another two took their place. Quill could feel the muscles in his sword arm numbing with fatigue, and sweat stung the nicks and cuts where the enemy had come close to ending him. He could hear the Duke's labored breathing, and could only shake his head in admiration—the older man was more than holding his own, showing no signs of giving way. But, despite the toll they were taking on the nomads, Quill knew it was only a matter of time before they fell.

A fresh wave of attackers surrounded them, their eyes burning with hatred and a healthy touch of caution as they gazed on the two men. In the brief lull, the Duke turned to Quill. "Well, Quill, this might be it for us," he gasped. "It's been an honor."

Quill forced a smile. "The feeling is mutual, sire, but it isn't over just yet."

He hoped that the words didn't sound as hollow to the Duke as they did in his own ears, but if they did, the Duke was gracious enough to pretend. Together they stood, waiting for the inevitable onslaught. The leader of the nomads raised his sword, but before he could bring it down in the signal to attack, there was an otherworldly shriek and a shadow blotted out the sun. Quill felt his heart lift as three of the winged beasts came swooping down, sending nomads tumbling left and right. As the creatures banked and came back for another run at the nomads, Quill blinked as three shapes detached themselves from the beasts' backs, tumbling through the air and landing among the massed ranks of the enemy.

In seconds, they were revealed to be warriors, leaping to their feet, and slashing and cutting through the enemy. One was unmistakably Gamora, sunlight flickering off of green skin as she ducked and weaved, blades shining in beautiful but deadly weaves of shining steel. Beside her, Ansari was a smaller version of Gamora, her fighting style showing the marks of her tutelage, and no less deadly for her young age. Quill frowned— who was the third figure? It was not quite as fast as the other two, but the way it wielded its sabre was more than a match for any of the nomads one on one. The fighting style was closer to the Duke's than Gamora's, more power than speed, and it was the older man who proved more perceptive than Quill.

"Karyn!" he yelled, fear and anger thickening his voice. "What are you doing here?"

The figure hesitated, almost falling victim to a nomad's vicious slash, then straightened and ran her opponent through.

"Father, now is not the time," Karyn yelled back. "Can't you see I am busy?"

Quill couldn't help but laugh, the Duke's glare doing little to quell his mirth. "You can't half tell she's your daughter," he said.

He stopped laughing a moment later at the Duke's barbed reply.

"I wouldn't say too much," he said. "I heard you two have unfinished business, and she looks much less forgiving than the nomads."

Quill swallowed, then fought his way to Gamora's side. "You were meant to be at the monastery keeping her safe," he said accusingly. He should have suspected something when they hadn't protested being shipped off. He had been so pre-occupied he had missed what was right in front of him.

Gamora chopped down another nomad before replying. "Did you really think that I would miss this battle?" she asked. "Since when do I need to be protected?"

"It's my home, too." The voice from beside Quill caused him to stumble, and it was only the speaker's slash across an attacking nomad's face that saved him. "Why shouldn't I be allowed to fight alongside all of the other men and women of the Duchy?"

"Karyn, I—" Quill stopped. "You're right. I'm sorry."

"You're still not my favorite person right now," Karyn replied, "but we can discuss that later. Right now, we have an empire to save."

Together, the warriors fought their way to the breach in the wall. The weight of numbers was starting to tell, but the Duke's arrival gave the defenders fresh heart, and they pushed the nomads back again and again. In one of the breaks between waves, the Duke tapped Quill on the shoulder.

"Do you see what I see?"

Quill peered through the breach, and swore. There, at the back of the enemy's lines, he could see dark figures gathering. It seemed that they had lost patience with the nomads' attempts to storm the castle, and were going to take a direct hand in matters. As they drew closer, the archers targeted them, remembering the damage they had done in the last battle. As arrows rained down upon them, Quill dared to hope for a moment, but that hope died stillborn in his breast as he watched the dark figures riding through the deadly hail. As they grew closer, Quill could see that many of them had arrows sticking out of them, as did their horses, but that didn't seem to be troubling them at all. As Quill watched, one reached up and pulled an arrow free from where it had buried itself between its eyes.

"What are they?" the Duke whispered.

"I don't know," Quill said. "But they aren't human."

There was more movement in the distance on the nomads' right flank, and Quill could only just make out another group of black figures approaching. There were perhaps two thousand of them, and though they were on foot, they were moving faster than a man could run.

"As if we didn't have enough problems," he said.

"What do you see?" the Duke asked.

Quill pointed out the movement, and the Duke stared at him, all at once looking like an old man.

"What have we done to deserve this, Quill?" he asked, voice trembling. "Why has everything turned against us?"

Quill had no answer for him, and instead, he watched the newcomers approach. Suddenly he straightened and grabbed the Duke's arm hard enough to make the older man wince.

"Actually, sire, I think things might have finally turned our way," Quill said.

At the head of the advancing army, Quill could now make out its leader, a hugely-muscled figure who took every step as if he owned the ground. Behind him followed a horde of his insectoid subjects, their shrill twittering filling the air.

"Sire, rally the men and get ready to charge forth. I have a feeling that our enemies are about to get a very nasty surprise."

The Duke seemed to shed his years in an instant, and was suddenly bellowing orders. Soldiers formed up behind him, knuckles white on the hilts of weapons already notched and battered with hard use.

"Men, this is your time. One last stand, and then glory!"

The men cheered, their shouts weary but full of conviction.

"I hope you know what you are doing, Lord Quill," the Duke said softly.

Quill clutched his sword tightly. "Sire, one way or another, we are about to find out."

CHAPTER 16

The nomads, unprepared for the ferocity of the onslaught, fell back in disarray as the Duke's soldiers charged. Quill and the Duke were the point of the spear that was aimed at the heart of the nomads' ranks. The Duke did not have Quill's technique, but he was tremendously strong, and he was fighting for his realm. Every time he swung his sword it bit deep into flesh. Because of the bottleneck, the fighting was too cramped for the nomads to bring their repeating bows into play, and one on one they were no match for the Duke's soldiers. Used to fighting on horseback, the nomads' swordsmanship was unsuited to the wild melee in which they found themselves. Furthermore, it was the most skilled of the Duke's men who had survived this long. They cut a red ruin through the invaders' ranks, and Quill could see that the nomads were shell shocked at the sudden reversal.

Despite the battle being on their side, Quill knew that it couldn't last. If they managed to break this wave of attackers, it would leave the defenders open to fire from the nomads' bows or—even worse—would allow the dark riders an open field for their own terrible charge. They were living on borrowed time, and Quill knew it.

"Lord Quill, what is your plan? We can't defeat them, not like this," the Duke yelled over the sound of the carnage around them. His sword arm was red to the elbow with blood and gore, and his eyes were wide and rolling with an almost berserker battle rage.

"We don't have to defeat them, sire," Quill yelled back. "We just need to distract them for a little longer."

Completely preoccupied with their siege, the nomads were unaware of the threat on their flank. As the last of the nomads at the walls fell, the dark riders formed up into ranks and prepared to charge. It was then that they finally became aware of the army approaching on their right. They wheeled to face it, but it was too late for them to build any momentum, as their enemy was already among them.

"Now!" Quill yelled, and raised his sword. "Let's roll the dice!"

Behind him, he heard a mighty roar as the Vylarans charged at the ranks of the nomads that had lined up out of bowshot while waiting for the dark riders to deal with the Duke's soldiers for them. The nomads were on the left flank of the riders, between them and the woods, and Quill's plan was to keep them occupied while their new allies dealt with the dark riders. He knew his men were the equal of any flesh and blood foe, but he wouldn't throw them away against an enemy that had showed it could crush them unless he had no choice. The nomads were the lesser of two evils.

The nomads were caught by surprise, obviously thinking that the Duke and his men had little fight left in them, and the men of the Empire set about showing the nomads just how wrong they were. Despite their momentary confusion, the nomads still had the advantage of numbers, however, and were fresher than the Duke's men. They refused to break, and slowly began to push back. Just as Quill was starting to worry that it was *his* men who would be routed, screaming sounded from the back of the nomads' ranks. Another force had emerged from the trees and was wreaking havoc among the nomads. A vast shout echoed across the battlefield.

"I am Groot!"

Quill could see Groot striding through the nomads' lines, simply sweeping them up with his vast arms and sending them tumbling away from him. Beside the giant marched files of axemen, methodically hewing down the enemy like so many saplings, their great axes sending sprays of blood and gore flying with every stroke. Quill recognized Barak among them, the huge man working such carnage that nomads began to flee from his approach. There were only a few hundred of the woodcutters, but their sheer viciousness demoralized the nomads and counted for more than mere numbers.

Something grabbed his leg, and Quill nearly stabbed it before he realized it was Rocket.

"Happy to see us, Quill?" Rocket shouted up at him, grinning like the little maniac he was.

"Happy? I could kiss you, but I'm worried about germs," Quill said. "How did you manage that? Barak wasn't very happy the last time I saw him."

Rocket gave a cagey look that made Quill nervous.

"I decided it was better to ask forgiveness than permission," he said. "If you were all dead, the Duke wouldn't care what promises I might have made in his name—and if you survived, he'd probably be too grateful to care."

"Oh no," Quill groaned. "Why do I get the feeling I might regret this? We'll discuss this further if we survive. Now, let's finish this."

He waved his men forward and they crashed into the nomad lines once more. Trapped between between troops hungry for revenge and the terrible axes of the woodcutters—not to mention the terror-inspiring figure of Groot—the nomads wavered. Finally, in a chain reaction of despair, they broke almost to a man, throwing down their weapons and fleeing for the trees. Those last few nomads too brave—or too stupid—to realize they were defeated fought on, but soon fell. The Duke's men raised their swords and cheered hoarsely.

"We aren't finished yet!" The Duke's bellow cut through the cheers.

In the heat of the battle, Quill had lost track of the secondary battle going on to his left. The dark riders refused to give up any ground, despite being outnumbered almost four to one. They could take incredible punishment, but the insectoids seemed to have come up with a strategy that was taking its toll. As Quill watched, one insectoid impaled a shadow figure with its slashing arms and held the struggling figure aloft while another used its primary arms to literally smash its enemy to pieces. All across the battlefield the insectoids were teaming up on the dark riders, and the ground was littered with their remains.

It was not all one sided, though, and Quill saw one of the dark riders carve his way through a dozen of the insectoids with a fiery sword before Drax grabbed its wrist and tore its arm from its body—then beat it to the ground with the limb itself. The dark riders were also using their mounts to their advantage. Whatever they were, they were rearing and lashing out with their hooves, while their riders slashed out with their swords. A number of the insectoids went down before they changed tactics and started targeting the steeds rather than riders, cutting their legs out from underneath them. It was brutal and it was cruel, but Quill had to admit it was effective.

With the nomads essentially destroyed as a cohesive fighting force, the Duke bellowed new orders at his men, forming them up into lines. There was an awkward moment when he came face to face with Barak and tried to order him to form up his axeman. For a moment Quill thought that Barak would refuse, but Rocket leaned down from his perch on Groot's shoulder and whispered in the big man's ear. Barak frowned, but then nodded curtly, and turned to his men.

"You heard the Duke, form up into a line. Let's not say that we were the weak link here today."

The Duke stared after him for a moment, and then gave Rocket and Groot a considering look before turning and walking back over to Quill.

"You certainly have some interesting friends, Lord Quill," the Duke said. "After this is over, if we are still alive, I will be very interested to learn more about them."

"First things first, sire," Quill replied. "Right now, don't you think we should go to the aid of those who are dying to defeat our enemies?"

"You're right, Lord Quill. I don't know what those . . . creatures are, but no one can fault their courage." He turned to the soldiers lined up behind him. "Men, you have already done more than anyone could fairly ask of you. You've bled for the realm, and your comrades have died. But there is still one more battle to fight. Will you follow me and wipe away this stain forever?"

"Yes!" The shout echoed from hundreds of throats as if they had but one great voice.

"Then, onwards!"

The Duke's men charged across the battlefield and crashed into the dark riders' flank. They had been watching the way the insectoids fought and attempted to follow suit. Swords slashed at the mounts' legs and many of them fell screaming. But the fiery swords also bit deep, and the Duke's men fell back, flesh and blood unable to stand against the unnatural strength and weapons of the invaders. The woodcutters had more luck—used to working in teams, they treated the riders like a particularly dangerous type of tree, taking turns with their axe strokes and cutting several down. But they, too, suffered under those terrible swords. Quill saw Edric topple backwards, sliced almost in half with one blow.

Despite their losses, the charge served its purpose. The attack had distracted the riders from the insectoids long enough for Drax and his subjects to regroup and seize the advantage. It was not long before the last of the dark riders was mere pieces scattered over the battlefield, and the last of their steeds put out of its screaming misery. The two armies met in the middle of the field and halted, lined up in rows and staring suspiciously at each other. Quill could hear soldiers talking behind him.

"What *are* those things? Are we going to have to fight them next?" one whispered far too loudly.

"I hope not, they look like tough buggers. And they did help us," his comrade replied.

"So? Look at them? Bugs are meant to be squashed."

"Silence!" the Duke roared. "No more talk like that or I will have you flogged, and that goes for anyone else. We'd all be dead—and the nomads would be looting the castle as we speak—if it weren't for them."

Quill was relieved. Blood was still running hot from the battle, and things had a way of getting out of hand at times like these. None of the other soldiers seemed to sympathize with the one who had drawn the Duke's ire, and most looked too exhausted to care about anything.

The Duke gestured to Quill, and together they walked out to the ground between the two armies, where Drax stood waiting. Quill reached out and clasped arms with him, wincing at the strength in the other man's grip.

"Thank you, Drax, you came through for us," Quill said. He turned to the Duke. "Let me make some introductions. Sire, this is Drax the Destroyer; Drax, this is the Duke of Vylara."

The two men gave each other measuring looks, but both must have approved of what they saw, and nodded in approval.

"The Empire owes you a debt of gratitude," the Duke said. "I thought that I was simply leading my men in a glorious but futile last stand, but you and your . . . men turned this into a victory that will be sung of for centuries."

"I do not abandon my friends, no matter what disagreements we might have had," Drax rumbled. "Your men fought bravely, but I am sorry I robbed you of the chance to die in glorious battle."

The Duke blinked in surprise at that, but Quill was used to Drax's strange notions.

"I think we can forgive you, Drax," Quill said. "I'm glad you changed your mind."

"It felt wrong letting you go off without my help," Drax replied. "I thought long and hard about what was the honorable thing to do, and I had resolved to follow you on my own, as I didn't feel right bringing my subjects to a war that was none of their concern. But when my advisors heard my plan, they wouldn't allow it, claiming that would dishonor them— and that where their king went, they went."

"And what is a man . . . or anyone, without honor?" the Duke said.

"Exactly! A man after my own heart," Drax said. "So we came to an agreement. If they helped my friends, I would abdicate the throne."

"You gave up your throne for us?" Quill asked, shocked. "I'm sorry, Drax."

Drax laughed. "Don't be, you know I was a reluctant king. I was not willing to give up the throne in the past because I felt it would devalue it to do so, but what is more valuable than honor and friendship? It seemed a fair price. Honor has been satisfied on both sides."

Quill shook his head. He was sure it made complete sense to Drax, but Quill knew he would never really understand.

"So, what now?" the Duke asked him. "How can I reward you?"

"All I would ask is that you recognize the sovereignty of my people, and sign a treaty with my successor pledging friendship and non-interference," Drax said. "They simply want to be left alone."

Quill could see the insectoid who had fought Drax standing

in the front row. It seemed that it had got its wish, after all.

"It would be my pleasure," the Duke said. "It is the least that I can do. And, what about you?"

"I think it is time I rejoined my friends," Drax said.

"I'm happy to hear that, Drax," Quill said. "Rocket and Groot are here, and Gamora will join us soon. I don't know what comes next—we're still stranded—but I'm convinced we're better off together."

"You will always have a place in my castle, Lord Quill. All of you," the Duke said. "That includes you, Lord Drax."

Drax bowed his head in thanks.

"Quill, we may not be as stranded as we thought," Drax said.

"What do you mean?"

"Have a look at the remains of the enemy."

Quill hurried over to the nearest corpse, bracing himself for the smells of death, but instead there were only the faint odors of ozone and hot metal. He pulled open the enemy's robe, and his mouth dropped open in shock. There was no blood—not even any flesh—just metal and plastics. Despite the fact that they had been pounded into fragments, he could make out the delicate tracery of high-end circuit boards.

"They're machines," Quill whispered. He knew what this meant, as did Drax.

"Where there is technology like this, there is likely to be

more," Drax said. "We may very well find what we need to repair our ship."

"Rocket! Groot! Get over here," Quill yelled.

Rocket was soon poking and prodding the corpses, looking for answers in their ruined workmanship.

"You know what? This is very advanced technology," Rocket said. "This sort of thing requires fabricators and refitting equipment. If we can find their base, I think we have a real chance of using it to repair the ship. I'll see if I can work out where they come from."

The Duke might not have understood much about the technology itself, but he was a long way from stupid.

"There will be survivors from the nomad army," he said. "I will make sure that they tell you everything they know."

"I suspect I have an idea of what they'll tell us," said Quill. He turned to Rocket. "I'm pretty sure we already know where they came from, along with that EMP."

"The shielded zone!" Rocket exclaimed. "Of course! If it isn't a natural phenomenon, it in itself is a sign of some pretty high-level tech."

"The problem is that we have no idea what we'll be walking into," Quill said grimly. "It possesses technology we don't, and it's deeply hostile to us and everything else on this planet."

Drax was the only one who seemed happy. "It should be fun!"

CHAPTER 17

"You can all go to hell."

The nomad spat on the floor in front of him, indifferent to the splendor of the Duke's audience chamber. The guard next to him turned and casually drove his fist into the captive's stomach, leaving him gasping for air.

"That will be enough of that," the Duke said. "There is no need for this to be difficult. We just want you to answer a few questions, and then you'll be sent back to the steppes."

"I've got nothing to say to you." The prisoner was a nondescript man, not particularly big, with a ratty beard. It was hard to believe he was one of the nomads that had almost brought the Empire to its knees. "I am no coward who spills his guts to the enemy."

"There is no point being stubborn. You can cling to your pride all you like, but you did surrender to us rather than die, so it all seems a bit empty."

That only made the prisoner glower even more, and the Duke sighed.

"I see this is useless. Take him away."

Quill cleared his throat. "If I may, sire?"

The Duke nodded and the guards dragged the captive

back in front of the dais where the Duke and his council were seated. Quill gestured for Rocket to join him.

"Look ferocious, and whatever I say, don't say a word, okay?" he whispered.

"What?" Rocket hissed back.

"Just do it." Quill turned back to the prisoner. "See this creature? Do you remember what happened on the battle-field? Did you see his vicious bloodlust?"

The prisoner nodded, his face going white. Rocket shot Quill a dirty look and then snarled at the prisoner, baring his teeth in an exaggerated grimace.

"He has a taste for human flesh now, and we haven't fed him today," Quill continued. "So, here's the deal. You're going to tell us everything we want to know, or . . ."

"Or?" the prisoner asked reluctantly.

"I'm going to get a really big sack, and then I'm going to bundle you and my pet here in it—and then we're going to whack it with sticks to get him all riled up." Rocket was snarling at Quill, who went on. "Or even more riled up."

"You wouldn't!"

"Guard, fetch me a sack!"

"No! I'll talk! Ask me anything."

Quill waved the guard away and leaned forward. "Tell me about the dark riders."

"About a year ago, a hooded figure visited my chieftain. We never saw his face—no one wanted to with the creepy way he talked and the way his eyes glowed red. But he impressed the chieftain when he easily killed our champion, and even more so when he brought gifts of armor and bows that fired faster and farther than anything we'd seen before. Then he started talking about invading the Empire and all the treasure we'd claim for ourselves. At first the chieftain said no, he didn't think we could win, but the stranger promised him an army and all the weapons we would need. He said all he wanted in return was to see the Empire knocked back to the Stone Age, whatever that means. It took a lot of persuading, as we knew that you had more soldiers and more weapons than we did, but he was extremely convincing."

The prisoner was stammering with fear and nerves by the time he trailed off.

"And where did he come from? Do you know?" Quill asked.

"Out of the Forbidden Lands. That's all I know, I swear!"

"The Forbidden Lands?"

"They are farther east. No one who goes in comes out."

Quill asked the man a few more questions, and then waved to the guards, who carried him almost weeping with relief from the hall.

As soon as he was gone, Quill started laughing and didn't stop until Rocket kicked him in the shins.

"You son of a . . ." Rocket said. "Your pet? A sack?"

"It worked, didn't it?" Quill said grinning.

"You're an evil man, Quill."

"Well done, Lord Quill," the Duke said. "Very sly. At least we know that the nomads are no threat to us on their own. I hope that we broke this mysterious enemy's strength in the last battle. But, we must deal with this forbidden place and make sure that it is no longer a threat."

"Sire, with all due respect, I think that you should leave that to my friends and me. It's more our specialty."

The Duke frowned. "I suppose that you have proved yourselves, but I don't like letting others fight my battles for me."

"Sire, we have our reasons to go there, too."

"So be it." The Duke signaled to his guards. "And now to the next order of business. Bring in the woodcutter, Barak."

Barak was not exactly a captive like the nomad, so his hands were unbound, but the two guards to either side of him kept their hands on the hilts of their swords.

"Sire." Barak barely inclined his head to bow, but the Duke ignored this.

"The realm is grateful for the bravery of you and your fellow woodcutters," the Duke said. "But the fact remains that you are poachers and outlaws, which leaves me with a dilemma. The laws regarding the forest are not just about protecting my resources and keeping them for myself. We have a treaty with another race, and my family is honor bound to protect them."

"We know that now." Barak's eyes slid to Groot and Rocket. "We've seen things that have convinced us. But it doesn't matter anymore. There is a giant wall around the forest and there is . . . something living in there, and none of my men will go near it."

"But you did in the past. You defied my authority."

"Yes, we did," Barak said, anger in his voice. "And I am not ashamed. I have a family to feed, and so do all my men. We just want a fair go."

Before the Duke could reply, Rocket broke in. "Sire, if I can speak?"

At the Duke's nod, he went on. "When you needed them, the woodcutters marched to your aid, even though they had seen many of their friends and comrades executed. All they asked in return was a fresh start, and rightly or wrongly we promised them amnesty. Not carte blanche to do whatever they wanted going forward—Groot would be very unhappy to see them cutting down those sentient trees—but a clean slate."

"You had no right to promise anything," the Duke said angrily.

Rocket didn't flinch at his tone, instead just met his gaze unblinkingly.

"Perhaps. But the fact is that we saved you, and I think you owe us for that—and you owe Barak and his men. What's more important, the good of your realm or your pride?"

Quill could see that Rocket had found the Duke's weakness, and that his words had hit home.

"I am not so closed minded as to not recognize truth when

I see it. Here is my decision. Barak, you are hereby named captain of my new Forest Guard, and given the rank of earl along with its requisite incomes. You are to recruit a force of men to uphold the treaty and protect the forest, and to serve the realm in times of war. Each man will be paid twice the average wage of a woodcutter. Do you accept this charge?"

"Y-yes, sire," Barak stammered.

"Know this—I reward good service. But if you take up this responsibility, I will expect you to be worthy of it. I will declare an amnesty for all those who poached wood, but from now on, anyone caught doing so will face the headsman. Is that fair?"

"More than fair, sire," Barak said. "I will wield the axe myself." He grinned.

The Duke didn't smile. "You've been given a great opportunity here. I trust you will be worthy."

Barak recognized a dismissal when he heard it, and this time he bowed before turning and leaving the audience chamber.

"I think that was well done, sire," Marius said. The Master of Arms had been gravely injured in the battle, and his head was swathed in bandages. But he had refused to rest, and had insisted on being at the audience.

"Perhaps, but where will we find the coin?" Tremas asked. He, too, had been injured. Quill had been surprised to hear that the older man had single-handedly killed half a dozen nomads, but he supposed you could never tell what a man was capable of.

"We will have many challenges over the next year," the Duke said. "There is much to be repaired and rebuilt. We will just have to do our best."

The other nobles nodded.

"So, Lord Quill, is there any boon that I can grant you?

"Sire, I don't think so. I'm just happy to be alive," Quill said. "All I really need is a way home, and I hope that we'll find that in these Forbidden Lands."

"I can't send you off without reward after the loyal service you have rendered, so I hope you will accept this small token."

At that signal, a servant rushed over, holding a long, thin bundle. The Duke took it and handed it to Quill, who unwrapped it.

"It's beautiful, sire."

It was a beautiful cavalry saber, with a hilt chased with silver and sapphires. When Quill pulled it from its sheath he whistled in admiration—it was perfectly balanced and razor sharp, made of some strange alloy.

"There have been many civilizations that have risen and fallen in our history. They get to a certain point and then some catastrophe brings them down. It is a recurring pattern that has puzzled us and inspired fear—will it happen to us? This is a relic from one of the kingdoms that rose higher than all the rest before it came crashing down."

"Thank you, sire," Quill said sincerely. "It is a truly noble gift."

"Are you sure that you won't stay?" the Duke asked, eyes

twinkling with amusement. "You could rise even further. I believe that my daughter would be happy if you stayed, too."

Quill coughed. "Thank you, sire, but my friends and I need to pursue a way to return to our home. I am honored by the suggestion, though."

The Duke reached out and clasped Quill's hand in his, squeezing hard enough that bones creaked.

"Thank you, Quill," the Duke said. "We will never forget what you have done for us."

With that, the travelers took their leave and headed for the stables, where Gamora and Karyn were waiting for them.

"Where's Ansari?" Quill asked.

"She has already left for the monastery," Gamora answered. "We'd said our goodbyes, and I don't think she wanted to draw them out."

"How did she take it?" he asked.

"Not well—she wanted to come with us. But I convinced her to stay at the monastery, that that was where she belonged," Gamora said. "I told her that she was ready to take my place, and that I knew she would be worthy."

"She did prove herself, didn't she?" Quill said.

"She gave me a message for you, too," Gamora said, smiling.

"What was that?"

"That the next time you see her she will be bigger and stronger—and that she will beat you easily."

"The young people of today . . . just no respect for their

elders," Quill said, laughing. He was touched, though, and it showed in his face as he turned to Karyn.

"Karyn, I'm glad to see you made it through safely," he said warily. He wasn't sure where they stood after the scene at his original departure, but he got his answer when she slapped his face, hard, before wrapping her arms around him and burying her head in his chest.

"Quill, I'll miss you." She looked up at him with tear-streaked eyes. "Don't forget me. Promise?"

Before he could do more than nod, she reached up and grabbed his hair, pulling his mouth down to hers. It was more than a few minutes before he could catch his breath and murmur in her ear.

"Never. I promise."

Quill was uncharacteristically quiet as they winged their way east. There were a lot of people he would miss from the Duchy, not only Karyn. He had been there only a few months, but they had gotten surprisingly deep under his skin. He looked around at his companions—at least he had them. Drax was now flying on what had been Ansari's beast, while the others had reclaimed their own. Quill patted the velvety softness of his mount's thorax with real affection. The beast was healing nicely after taking a number of arrows during his rescue of the Duke. It had proved a brave and loyal steed.

"Are you okay, Quill?" Gamora yelled across the gap between them.

"I'm fine, Gamora, just thinking about friendships and goodbyes, and how hard they are."

"I will miss my sisters at the monastery," she replied. "It's bittersweet saying goodbye. I am happy knowing that I have made a difference in their lives, though—and they in mine. I guess that's all you can do when you have to say goodbye— keep the memory burning brightly in your heart against the day that you meet again."

"Do you think we'll ever return here?" he asked.

"I hope so," Gamora said. "But we have to get off the planet first. If we do, then it won't be hard to come back, as we have the coordinates now."

"That's true," Quill said. "And isn't there a finder's fee for discovering a new planet? Maybe we'll recoup our losses after all!"

"One can only hope," Gamora laughed. "That will go a long way to improving everyone's opinion of you after that last escapade."

"It seems so long ago now," Quill said. "I'd almost forgotten our argument."

"I guess we've been reminded of what is really important over the last few weeks," Gamora said. "Friendship is too precious to just throw away."

"Are you two being mushy again?" The voice was right in

his ear, and Quill nearly screamed. He looked up to see Rocket's grin only feet from his own. The raccoonoid had his beast flying inverted right above Quill, and he was hanging upside down. "But, yeah, this is much more fun than when we're yelling at each other, isn't it? Besides, check your saddlebags."

Quill stuck his hand in his bag and found it full of gold coins.

"A little present from the Duke," Rocket said. "I didn't tell you until now because I didn't want you doing something stupid—like trying to turn it down."

"Well, if we can just get our ship fixed, this little adventure might turn out to be rather profitable," Quill said.

"That's the way I like my adventures," Rocket said. "But we'll find out soon enough whether it's possible." He pointed down to where the ground had changed color from the dull tan of the steppes to a melancholy grey. "There's the beginning of the Forbidden Lands."

CHAPTER 18

The Forbidden Lands made the land around the Broken Hills look positively welcoming. The soil was grey and lifeless, and there were no trees to provide shade from the unforgiving sun. On a planet that had impressed them with its sheer pleasantness, this place was an anomaly. The only thing that broke the monotony of the horizon was a towering shape in the distance—and that was where they were headed, one step at a time. They had seen if from the air—a huge ovoid shape that looked like nothing more than a giant, matte-steel egg standing upright on its base. It was perhaps three hundred feet tall, with the same general proportions of a chicken's egg. It stood out from the nothingness of the land around it like a sore thumb, and seemed the natural place to start exploring. Rocket had suggested that just flying straight towards it might not be the best option in case it possessed unpleasant defensive measures—and remembering the battle with the invaders, the rest had agreed—but after hours of walking, Quill was starting to regret that decision.

By the time they were close enough to be in the egg's shadow, it was late afternoon. They stopped for a brief drink and then checked their weapons. Gamora and Rocket had each liberated one of the nomads' repeating bows. They were well designed—a crossbow rather than a longbow, with a hollow stock that held a magazine containing twenty bolts. The weapons, using a cunning counterweight system to recock the action, could fire almost as fast as gun. Rocket and Gamora both carried extra magazines, and they each also had a close-in weapon—Gamora her ubiquitous knives, and Rocket the cudgel he had used to good effect in the forest. Drax had claimed one of the fallen woodcutters' axes, and like any weapon, it seemed designed to fit in his hand. Quill was content with the beautiful blade the Duke had given him. He wondered how it would look with the gear he had back at the ship. Dashing, unless he was mistaken.

It was eerily quiet, and nothing stirred at their approach. As the egg grew closer, they could make out a flight of stairs leading up to an open hatchway. Strangely, the stairs seemed to be a newer addition, constructed from wood rather than the same metal as the egg.

"You know what this is, right?" Rocket asked.

"It's a spaceship, isn't it?" Quill replied.

"Yes, and if play our cards right, then not only do we get salvage rights, it might be our way home," Rocket said.

"Well, the latter is much more important than the former," Gamora said. "And let's not take anything for granted."

They slowly ascended the steps, testing each one before putting their feet down fully. They needn't have worried, as the staircase was well put together and seemed in very good repair. In this dry and desiccated climate, that indicated regular maintenance. However, despite the stairs' indication otherwise, the interior of the egg had the desolate feel of a place that had been empty for far too long. It was nothing quantifiable, just the aura a place gets when nothing living had walked its halls for decades or more. It gave Quill the creeps.

Despite that, everything inside still ran smoothly. The first time an air extractor kicked in, Quill jumped about a foot in the air, but the breeze that wafted through corridors was perfect—clean and fresh. Lights came to life as they walked down empty corridors, all the bulbs shining brightly, none flickering or dead.

"This is like a haunted house," Quill said to Gamora. "I keep waiting for someone to jump out and scream 'Boo!'"

"What's a haunted house?" she asked, confused.

"Never mind," he muttered, and kept walking. Sometimes, he forgot that he was among aliens, and that the things he took for granted were mysteries to them—and vice versa. It reminded him of how far he was from home, even before they had passed through the anomaly.

They came to a bank of elevators and stopped.

"Should we risk it?" Rocket asked.

"Everything else seems to be running perfectly well," Gamora said. "This ship is in better shape than Quill's ever was, and it is certainly much cleaner."

"Hey!" Quill said, but without any real heat. He couldn't really argue with her on that.

The buttons in the elevator were inscribed with an unfamiliar alien script that was all hooks and lines. Even Gamora, whose esoteric knowledge constantly amazed Quill, couldn't identify it. But that didn't faze them. Quill simply hit the uppermost floor, assuming that was where they would find the control room. If not, they weren't in any huge hurry. There was a faint sensation of weightlessness as the elevator began to move, and the display over the door began to glimmer. Each of the floor buttons lit up in turn, blinking faster and faster. When they stopped, though, it wasn't on the top floor but the one below it. No matter how many times Quill pressed the button, the elevator wouldn't go any farther. He shrugged and pressed the button that had a universally recognizable symbol for open, and they stepped out.

They found themselves in an open chamber that stretched from hull to hull with no internal walls or partitions. It was dotted with what looked like space-age coffins standing upright. As the travelers approached, a low-pitched humming began to emanate from the coffins.

"I really don't like this," Rocket muttered.

Around him, the other travelers tensed, hands clenched around their weapons.

"You're not the only one, buddy," Quill said. "I've got a bad feeling about this."

The humming built to a crescendo, the high-pitched whining causing the companions to clamp their hands over their ears. There was a final electronic shriek, and then red lights started to flash on the tops of a number of the coffins. With a sound of hydraulics, the coffins hissed open, revealing their contents.

"Oh, crap," Rocket said.

Once their robes had been removed, the nature of the dark riders had become apparent—but seeing them unveiled and still moving was something else again. Slowly, rows of dark figures rose from their metal wombs, their silence serving to add to the feeling of menace that oozed from them in almost tangible waves. The figures were robots built along bipedal lines, but their limbs and torsos seemed more elongated than a normal human's, as if they had been melted slightly and stretched out by a giant pair of hands. They were made from a silvery metal polished to a high sheen, and ribbed. Their heads were egg-shaped—the ship on a much smaller scale—and red, glowing eyes gave them a sinister aspect. One or two of them were oddly incomplete—one missing a hand, another a big section of paneling on its torso, revealing its inner workings.

Quill realized that this must be where the dark figures were fabricated, and that these were the replacements for the machines that had been destroyed in the battle for the castle. It seemed that they had arrived just in time. If the robots could be built this quickly, there could be another army standing before the castle walls within weeks. Quill counted four dozen pods, almost half of which were still closed, pregnant with the menace of their contents. He wondered how close they were to bearing their deadly offspring.

There was the thrum of the bows, and arrows started flying past Quill as Gamora and Rocket fired at the robots. Bolts ricocheted off their armor with a trail of sparks, or clattered to the ground at their feet, leaving the robots unmarked as they continued to move towards the companions. Then one robot staggered back as smoke poured from its eyes.

"The eyes!" Quill yelled. "Aim for the eyes."

Another robot went down, a bolt in each eye, and then the robots were in among them. They didn't carry swords, but they didn't need them—they were living weapons. The robots used their arms like clubs, raining down blows on Drax, Groot, and Quill as they sought to give Gamora and Rocket time to use their bows to their best advantage. Drax was willing to go toe to toe with them, swinging his axe in terrible arcs that sheered through metal as if it were flesh, but Quill didn't have that option. He feinted and ducked under blows that would have shattered bone, and lashed out with his sword. He nearly dropped it when it hit its first target and began to vibrate in his hand, sliding through the steel like a hot knife through butter.

"What a sword!" he yelled gleefully to Drax. "It must have been designed to fight these things."

"Their kingdom may have fallen before these creatures," Drax replied, "but be the instrument of their revenge as you wield their legacy."

It was a bit flowery, but Drax had a point. Quill silently thanked the Duke and whoever had forged this blade, and waded into the melee. It was hard to keep an eye on how his companions were faring—the robots were too dangerous to not get his full attention—but out of the corner of his eye he saw Groot halt the charge of one of the robots with a hand to its chest that stopped it in its tracks. The robot shuddered, and then roots and tendrils grew out of its mouth and eyes and it screamed with a terrible electronic shriek.

"I am Groot!"

Gamora had stopped shooting and had now drawn her knives. She was too quick for even the hyper reflexes of the machines, and she knew exactly how to use their strength against them. As one threw a punch, she caught the inside of its arm, pivoted, and sent it flying into one of the other robots, leaving them on the ground in a writhing tangle of limbs. Before they could extricate themselves, she had sunk a dagger up to the hilt in an eye each, and they went limp. Beside her, Drax swung his axe as if he were the machine, and was surrounded by a pile of metallic limbs. Unlike human foes, an amputation didn't put the robots out of the fight though, so every few blows would see Drax splitting a skull down the middle like it was a log he was getting ready for the fire.

Any time one of the off-worlders looked like they might be overwhelmed, there would be the hiss of a bolt, and their attacker would stagger back clutching an eye. The bolts weren't always enough to destroy whatever passed for a brain, but they would disorient the robot enough that it was easy pickings. Rocket's pinpoint accuracy and ice-cold nerves cost the robots dearly, and Quill could feel the battle turning against their foes. His sword seemed to sing with exultation as it vibrated through metal, every blow doing as much damage as Drax's powerful axe strokes. But just as Quill thought they were on the brink of victory, lights began to flash on the tops of the unopened coffins, and there was an ominous hiss as the doors began to open.

There was something odd about the robots that emerged, and it took Quill a moment to figure it out. These ones were incomplete, unfinished, the last desperate roll of the dice of whatever was controlling them. One was blind, with empty sockets where the red glow of eyes should have been, and it shuffled towards them with arms extended, terrible and piti-ful at the same time. Another had no legs, and dragged itself along the floor by clawing into the metal and pulling itself one agonizing yard at a time. Another should have been funny to watch, hopping on one leg towards them, but its implacable sense of purpose drained all humor from the sight. These robots were dealt with easily enough, but there was no sense of celebration in it.

Finally, the last of the robots collapsed to the deck, nearly split in two by a terrible blow from Drax's axe. Bits and pieces of robot were scattered everywhere, some still trying to move. A severed arm clutched at Quill with blind urgency, clawed hand opening and closing with malevolent greed. Quill shuddered as he kicked it away from him, and stepped around a head that stared at him and mouthed silent threats.

"Is this what the haunted houses you spoke of are like on your planet, Quill?" Gamora asked.

"Slightly fewer homicidal robots," he replied. "But more vomiting children."

Gamora made a face. "That's disgusting."

The companions made a point of going to each coffin and ensuring that it was empty, levering open the doors to reveal its contents. In some there was simply a head or a torso, unable to move and come out to attack. These they destroyed, not knowing whether they might grow into something more dangerous. Quill couldn't help but feel a bit guilty at demolishing the helpless automatons, but he consoled himself with the thought that they weren't really alive. It wasn't that he was squeamish, it was just that killing was something you couldn't take back, and he avoided it as best he could.

While they were finishing off the last of the robots, Rocket had been examining the machinery connected to the coffins. He let out a yelp of excitement and rushed over to Quill.

"Finally, some good news!" he exclaimed. "There are enough

parts here for me to fabricate what we need and repair the ship! As long as you have that system backup and we can scavenge a crystal array, we could be heading home within a week."

"And if there is no crystal array?" Quill asked.

"Then I'll grow a new one. That will take months, though— maybe three or four."

"Still better than years," Gamora said.

"Before we go, we have some unfinished business," Drax said. "We need to find out who is controlling this ship. We can't just take what we want and leave—otherwise it might just start all over again."

Quill had a terrible mental image of the castle in flames, dark riders swarming across the Empire.

"You're right, Drax. We have to finish what we've started. We can't leave our friends with the threat of another army hanging over their heads."

The rest nodded. They had all made friends on this planet, and were determined to do the right thing by them.

Rocket pointed to the spiraling staircase in the center of the room. Like the one outside, it was made of wood, as if it hadn't been part of the ship's original design.

"That looks like it goes up to the control room, and I'm certain that's where we'll find some answers," he said. "I'm just glad that whoever—or whatever—is up there hasn't emerged yet to blow us full of holes. Anyone who owns a ship like this must have a blaster pistol or two."

"Maybe they are waiting for us to stick our heads up so they can blow them off," Gamora said.

"Or maybe they are huddled in the corner sobbing because they know that we are coming for them," Drax rumbled. "They should be scared, too. I am going to have words with them. With my fists, I mean."

"Thanks for clarifying that, Drax," Quill said, winking at Gamora. "I don't see what choice we have. We'll just have to be cautious, like always."

Gamora coughed, almost choking as she tried not laugh.

"Okay, let's go," Quill said.

They ascended the stairs as stealthily as possible, trying to avoid alerting whatever it was that might be waiting for them.

CHAPTER 19

The control room was almost as big as Quill's entire ship. It had a number of comfortable-looking benches centered around a massive holo projector, and what looked like a conference table surrounded by luxurious chairs. The whole of what Quill had mentally assigned as the front half was taken up by the bridge. This was no single-pilot job, but a serious piece of spacecraft that would require a crew of about a dozen. In a pinch, Quill supposed that one person could have piloted it alone by assigning the crew functions to the ship's computer, but there was always something lost with that approach—an indefinable quality that meant the difference between a passable voyage and a good one. Quill much preferred his own ship and didn't have to rely on anyone else to fly it, though he had to admit that he had grown used to having someone to spell him when he wanted a break. But that was a luxury, not a necessity, like it came close to being here.

As he would have expected, the bridge was centered on the looming presence of the command chair, which looked out over the other stations and had the best view of the massive screen that ran all the way around the circular room. Directly in front of the bridge was a bank of controls, but Quill knew that each of the chairs would have its own console, and that the command chair would be able to override them all. Right now the screen was set to transparent, so the travelers could look out in a 360-degree angle over the Forbidden Lands—not that there was much to see. At least the stars were beautiful, glowing brighter than any Quill had seen on planets where industry polluted the sky and dimmed the heavens' light. The two moons were both full, the smaller one just starting to overlap the larger.

The others were still checking out the lounge area. Groot stood sentry, watching out for any further surprises, while Gamora was lying back with her feet up. Rocket and Drax were playing a game that looked a lot like foosball, but that had weird alien creatures instead of football players, and a ball that looked like a tetrahedral crystal that, every so often, would move in ways that defied the laws of physics. Quill kept walking, past the chairs and up to the front of the room. The fact that the whole wall was perfectly transparent gave the disconcerting impression that you could walk right over the edge and fall from the ship to the ground far below. Quill walked up to it, and nerved himself to run his hands over the surface. He felt a bit of vertigo as he reached out, half expecting his hand to go right through, but instead, felt only the cool hardness of the screen.

He turned to join his friends and jumped backwards in shock, his back coming up hard against the screen and scaring the life out of him when his eyes gave him the message that he was leaning back against empty air. He straightened, heart hammering in his chest from both nasty shocks, as he took in the sight in front of him. From the back, the command chair had looked empty but now he could see that it, alone of all the seats on the bridge, still had an occupant. The desiccated corpse was slouched in its seat, which was why its head hadn't been visible from behind. It was perfectly preserved, and Quill deduced that there must be an air filtering system still running that removed all bacteria from the ship. However, the dry air had sucked all the moisture from the corpse, and it was mummified and shrunken.

The corpse's shriveled condition made it hard to assess how big it would have been when it was alive, but Quill guessed it would have been about his height and build—but that was where the similarities ended. Its face was a mass of tentacles that hung down over its chest. Some had snapped off and lay on the ground at the base of the chair, but most were still intact. It had one huge eye in the middle of its forehead, which looked like it was all pupil with just a narrow band of red iris around the edge. What could be seen of its skin was a dull, greenish color, and it had no nose—just nostrils set flush into its face. Its arms ended in more tentacles, ranging from the thickness of a pencil to one as thick as Quill's wrist.

The cause of death wasn't hard to determine—a terrible wound to its stomach had spilled its intestines onto its lap, and its left hand still clutched them in a desperate attempt to hold them in. Quill had a mental image of the creature—no, the person—in the chair facing some calamity, struggling to pilot a ship that was supposed to have dozens of crew members on his own, all the while in terrible agony and feeling his life slipping away. Or, Quill supposed, he could have been some tyrannical captain whose oppressed crew had mutinied, forced him to land here, and then killed him before slipping away. But Quill liked to give everyone the benefit of the doubt—even long-dead aliens who had sent killer robots to destroy neighboring civilizations. Some people saw it as a character flaw; he saw it as a virtue. Whatever had happened, he or she—or it—was not a direct threat. Or so he hoped.

"Guys, I think you need to come over here," he called out.

"Hang on, I've got Drax on the ropes," Rocket yelled.

"Ropes? There are no ropes," Drax said. "And I will be victorious."

"I think you should come over here, *now*," Quill said.

He could hear them grumbling, but they came anyway. They gathered around him and stared at the alien corpse.

"Wow, someone wasn't messing around," Rocket said. "They wanted him dead."

"That's a bad way to die," Drax said. "He might have lingered for hours, even days, if shock and blood loss didn't kill him. I know, I have seen it."

Quill didn't ask whether Drax had inflicted it. He wasn't sure he wanted to know the answer.

"He has been dead a very long time," Gamora said. "So, who's been sending the robots and stirring up the nomads, then?"

"Very good question," Quill said. "It's a bit hard to stop someone who is already dead."

"Let's see whether they left any clues," Rocket said.

He waddled over to the computer and started punching buttons, muttering as he worked his way through the alien command hierarchy. As always, Quill could only admire the raccoonoid's intuitive genius when it came to technology, and the way he played it like an instrument rather than an unfeeling machine. After a few minutes, Rocket cursed under his breath and kicked the base of the screen. It must have hurt, because he started dancing around and cursing, this time not so much under his breath. When he had calmed down he turned back to the others.

"It's locked down pretty tight. But I think there's a way around it, though it's not pretty," he said. "Gamora, can you give me a hand, please?"

"Sure, what would you like me to do?"

"Sorry, I meant can you give me one of those hands?" She looked at him blankly, and then he clarified. "Tentacles! Can you take your knife and cut off one of those hands with the tentacles and give it to me?"

"Oh, gross, Rocket!" Quill said. "Is that really necessary?"

"Well, unless you have another way to break this encryption without using the handprint scanner, yes, it's necessary."

Wordlessly, Gamora pulled out her knife and began to saw through the dead pilot's wrist. In a few seconds she had cut the tentacle free, marched over to Rocket, and slapped it down in his outstretched paw.

"Thanks, Gamora," he said cheerfully. "That wasn't so bad, was it?"

When she didn't answer, he shrugged and returned to the computer system. He placed the hand, palm down, on a sensor and with a soft chiming the screen came to life.

"Now, let's see what we can find out." After a few minutes he let out a soft whistle, and punched in another command, the alien symbols becoming recognizable to them all. "Well, well, well."

"What is it, Rocket?" Quill asked.

"Whoever he or she or it was, they weren't stupid," Rocket said. "What would you do if you were on the run and needed to lay low?"

"I don't know, find somewhere where no one could find me, or would even come looking for me?"

"Exactly, and that's exactly what it did. It found a planet that wasn't even on the charts, with no technology to speak of. That meant that no one on the planet would have any idea it was here, and the chances of Nova Corps or some scouting parting stumbling across it would be extremely low," Rocket said. "But do you want know the really clever part?"

"I am sure you are going to tell us," Drax said.

Rocket was so excited that he ignored the barb.

"This pilot is a member of a very long-lived race—I'm talking millennia. It was going to hole up here for a long time until the heat died down, but it didn't want the locals progressing too far and doing things like sending out radio signals or space probes. That might have attracted attention, and it wasn't going to allow that."

"So, what, every time a civilization got close to a certain point, it would engineer something to set them back a few centuries?" Gamora asked. "That's not clever, that's evil."

"True, but it's also very elegant. Quill, didn't the Duke say their histories were littered with societies that got to a certain point and then mysteriously collapsed?"

"Yes, and we saw signs of it ourselves in the mountains," Quill said.

"Well, here's your culprit. Kind of. Indirectly."

"What do you mean by that?" Quill asked.

"Something went wrong with its getaway and it was injured. Badly, as you can see," Rocket said. "Its last action was to set the ship on course here and program in the instructions for the ship's computer. Any civilization that got to a certain point was to be destabilized, but no technology beyond them was to be used in case it attracted attention. That's why we saw better bows, armor, and weaponry, but no blast rifles or attack aircraft. Even the fiery swords were likely some sort of illusion, and the robots were disguised. If the Nova Corps had landed here, they wouldn't have found anything in the history books that would have given it away."

"That's genius," Quill said, simultaneously admiring the plan and being horrified by it.

"Yeah, shame it didn't make it to the cryonic healing chamber before the wound killed it," Rocket said. "So, its body has been sitting there for two-and-a-half thousand years while the computer has been following its final order. No malice, no hatred, just cold obedience."

"Can you shut it down?" Quill asked.

"Already done. Their long watch is over, and now the planet's evolutionary progress can resume its rightful course."

"To think all this was caused by an intergalactic fugitive who never even saw the damage he was doing," Gamora said.

"There is one piece of good news, though," Rocket said. "Really good news."

He grinned at them all, waiting for someone to ask.

"I am Groot?"

"Well, big guy, this particular fugitive had a very big bounty on its head. Very big. And it's the kind that doesn't expire, because its race is still around—maybe even some of the ones who were after him. So when we get back to civilization, we're all going to pocket a nice big piece of change."

"How big?" Gamora asked.

Rocket named a figure and their eyes widened.

"It looks like I'm going to Sin after all," Rocket gloated. "And I plan on breaking the bank while I'm there. I'll certainly have myself a decent stake to get started."

"Wow," Quill said. "So, I guess in the end, my little adventure served the greater good. You're all welcome."

"What?!" Gamora said. "How do you figure that?"

"Well, if we hadn't been fleeing an angry father, we wouldn't have stumbled into that anomaly, and we wouldn't have come here," Quill said. "And it's good that we did. After all, we not only saved a whole planet, but made some good money while doing it." He smiled smugly. "This is why I am the leader."

In retrospect, Quill decided he should have waited to make sure they didn't have anything to throw at him before he laid out those home truths. It took weeks for the tetrahedral-shaped mark between his eyes to fade.

EPILOGUE

Quill sat in his pilot's chair, looking out at the glittering nebula. The computer told him that in fifteen minutes the anomaly would be in the correct alignment to take them back to known space in a fraction of the time it would take to find the right coordinates for a warp-drive jump. But right now, he was enjoying simply relaxing for the first time in what seemed like an eternity. All was well with his world. Rocket had scavenged enough parts from the alien ship to not only completely repair his ship, but to put it in the best shape it had been in since he had . . . borrowed it. They'd also collected the evidence they needed to claim the bounty, so soon his bank balance would be in the black for the first time in years. It was a good feeling not to be worrying about his ship breaking down, or how he would pay for the repairs if it did. But that was only part of his sense of complete satisfaction.

There was a movement next to him as Gamora slid into the copilot's chair.

"You look very happy, Quill. What are you thinking about?"

He stayed silent for a moment, trying to work out how to put it into words.

"There's an old Earth song that says you don't know what you've got 'til it's gone. It's a cliché, but it's true. Sometimes you don't appreciate what you have until you no longer have it," he said. "I didn't realize quite how much I'd come to rely on you all until you all left me. It's made me think about things—the way I act sometimes."

"I think we all do things, and say things, we regret later," Gamora said. "But it's good that you are thinking about that sort of thing. Self-awareness is sign of growing up."

"I don't want to grow up," Quill laughed. "I'm having far too much fun the way I am. But, I'm happy that we're all back together again. I missed you guys."

She smiled at him and then stared out the window.

"Do you think they will be okay?" she asked. "Ansari, the sisters, Karyn, and the Duke. All of them?"

Quill thought about all of the people they had left behind.

"I don't know, Gamora," he said. "There are no guarantees in life—not for anybody. But now they'll be able to live the lives they were meant to live, with no interference. I guess that's all you can really ask for in this life."

"I guess so," she said.

The computer beeped, and Quill looked down at the display.

"Looks like it's time to go," he said. "Ready for the next adventure?"

"That's not the question. Now that we're back together, is the next adventure ready for *us*?"

Quill grinned and hit the button. There was a lurch, and then the ship disappeared from real space, on its way to its next destination.

Acknowledgments

Thank you to George and Parris, the Minions, and all of my friends in the Brotherhood Without Banners (who have so patiently listened to me incessantly talk about writing all these years) for your support, belief, and encouragement over the past decade. Without you, I wouldn't have gotten this far.

A special thanks to Jasmine and Nichole for reading an early version and for making me believe I was on the right track, as well as to Paul, Steffie, Rebecca, and all the other amazing people at Joe Books for their hard work in getting this book ready.

If I were to list everyone who has given me their time and support since I submitted my first short story, it would be a book in itself. I hope you know who you are, and how much you mean to me. But, special thanks go to Bob Greenberger, Cat Sparks, Jack Dann, Jason Fischer, and Tehani Wessely for taking the time to mentor and encourage me.

To my family, without whose love and support my dreams of being published would still be just dreams. Thank you for believing in me, and for your patience with all of the times I locked myself away in my study.

This book was written with the help of Scrivener and Dropbox, two of the best friends a writer can have.

ABOUT THE AUTHOR

David McDonald is a mild-mannered editor by day, and a wild-eyed writer by night. Based in Melbourne, Australia, he works for an international welfare organization, and divides his spare time between playing cricket and writing.

In 2013 David won the Ditmar Award for Best New Talent, and in 2014 won the William J. Atheling Jr. Award for Criticism or Review and was shortlisted for the WSFA Small Press Award. His short fiction has appeared in anthologies from publishers such as Moonstone Books, Satalyte Publishing, Crazy 8 Press, and FableCroft Publishing. In 2015, his first movie novelization, *Backcountry*, was released by HarperCollins.

David is a member of the Horror Writers Association, The International Association of Media Tie-In Writers, and the Melbourne based writers group, SuperNOVA.

You can find out more at

http://www.davidmcdonaldspage.com